Felix Publishing 2019
email: info.felixpublishing@gmail.com
Print copies available from publisher.

The Ice Ship

2019 digital book
release ISBN:
978-1-925662-27-6
Illustrated Print Edition
ISBN: 978-1-925662-26-9
Author: P. T. Scott
Registration:
Thorpe-Bowker +61 3 8517 8342
email: bowkerlink@thorpe.com.au

This is a work of fiction. The characters in this book did not exist and the practices of the time have been generalized. Most of the places described are real and have been visited by the author.

Illustrations by the author

The Ice Ship

Peter T Scott

To my grandchildren who are yet to
travel to their own faraway places

Also by the Author

Non-fiction:
  Adventures in Earth Science series:
  (as Dr. Peter T. Scott)

> *Exploration Science*
> *Riches from the Earth*
> *Changing the Surface*
> *Rocks – Building the Earth*
> *Fossils – Life in the Rocks*
> *A Dangerous Planet*
> *Through Sea and Sky*
> *Beyond Planet Earth*

and the composite textbook and companion books:

> *Adventures in Earth Science*
> *Adventures in Earth Science Practical Manual*
> *Adventures in Earth Science Teachers' Guide*

Also:

> *Adventures in Earth and Environmental Science*, Books 1 & 2 and their companion laboratory manuals and Teachers' guide.

Fiction: (as Hernan Moreno Ruiz)
> *Letters from San Rafael*

Contents

Foreword by the Author

This is a work of total fiction but many of the places and some of the events are real and of my own experience. I do not condone the commercial whaling industry and would be happy if it was disbanded, allowing only the few indigenous peoples to hunt them in their traditional manner. However, I needed an excuse for a 19th Century ship to be in Antarctic waters and so I made it a whaler. The story is based upon my experiences in Antarctica in a small, former research vessel in which I travelled in 2011. You can relive my trip by watching the video at:

https://www.youtube.com/watch?v=5t1gqad0554&list=PL137yCprodWD5_OI75T7vRDUgqhbcUO0A

I have also been trained at sea in square-rigged ships, although my voyages were in warmer climes along the eastern Australian coast. Come sailing with me at:

https://www.youtube.com/watch?v=ohaVjUrLN3M

Antarctica is a totally awesome environment but hostile to mankind and I have attempted to show what it would be like to have to work and be alone in such a place.

Dr. Peter T. Scott
2019

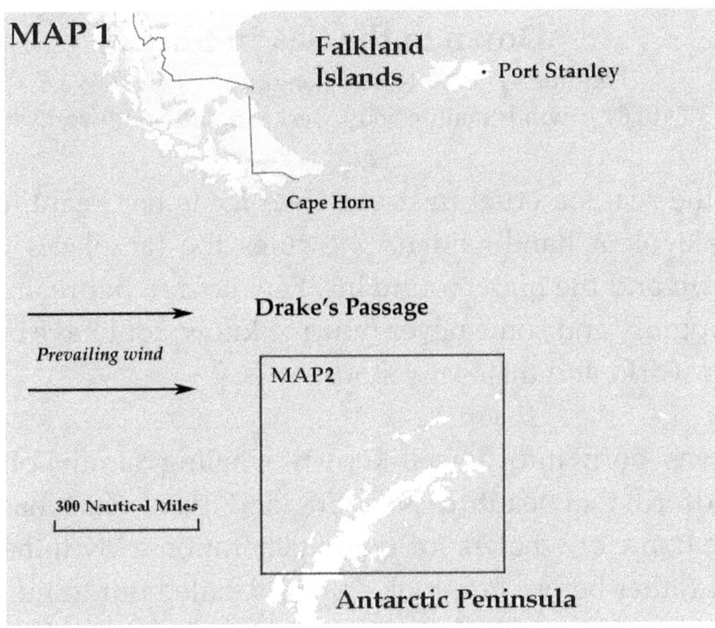

MAP 1
Falkland
Islands
Port Stanley
Cape Horn
Drake's Passage
Prevailing wind
MAP2
300 Nautical Miles
Antarctic Peninsula

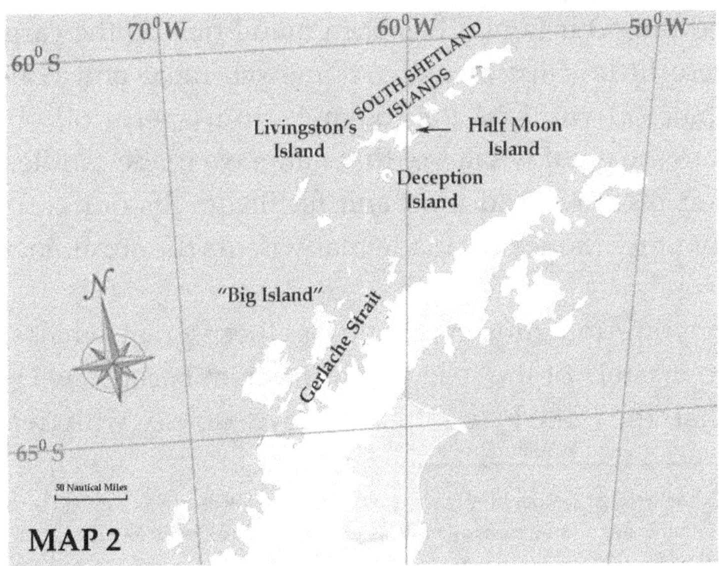

70°W
60°W
50°W
60°S
SOUTH SHETLAND
ISLANDS
Livingston's
Island
Half Moon
Island
Deception
Island
"Big Island"
Gerlache Strait
N
65°S
50 Nautical Miles
MAP 2

Chapter One
Down to the Sea in Ships

Latitude 41°39′06″North; Longitude 70°56′01″West
23⁰F¹ to 64⁰F, winds mainly Southwest to South Southwest variable

If the sea is a cruel mistress, then ice is her beautiful but malevolent handmaiden. She rules the far places of the Earth and the high mountains. Few go into her realm with impunity and some never return. I know; for I have been to her world and this is my story.

I was born into a well-known whaling family of New Bedford; that beautiful New England town which has been the home of whalers for many generations. My father and his father before him took ship and sailed out to hunt and capture the great whales of the Atlantic in weathers foul and fair. Our family has been made rich on the cargoes of these little ships bringing home oil, meat and bone. The whale oil we used for cooking; from sperm oil obtained from the great whales of that name we made candles; from their meat we had food and fertilizers for our crops; and from their bones we made many items for our homes.

They are magnificent creatures, these great whales; truly the masters of the seas. We hunt them because we needed what they have to offer but we do so with fear and

---

¹ The Fahrenheit temperature scale is used in this book as it was and still is used in the United States. Conversion to Celsius (Centigrade) is by C = 5/9(F - 32) e.g. 64⁰F = 5/9 (64-32) = 18⁰C.

reverence. Some whales are easy prey and flee from our harpoons. Others are fierce and will destroy the small whale boats and their crew which hunt them. Aye, and they have been known to attack the mother whaling ship as well and sink them below the sea.

So this is my story of how the search for the great whale led my ship and its crew far away from our beloved North American shore and into a treacherous world of wind and ice.

I am James, born in 1820, the only son of Captain Abraham Tobey, one of New Bedford's most famous whaling captains.

In the town and at sea my father was always called the 'Captain' as it was the custom in the family to do so as well. He could be a hard man at times but I believe that he loved my two sisters and I, although it was his creed not to show it. In time he took me to sea to learn his trade. First, at age twelve I was his Cabin Boy and did whatever book learning I could in the great cabin aft and also my seaman's skills on the open deck above. Below, my teachers were the great books of literature, the classics of the Ancient Greeks and books of mathematics and geography. Above I had many able teachers to show me the skills and secrets of the sailor man: knots and splices; the handling of sails; the use of the sextant and maps and the ways of the sea and the sky. Of course, the other duties of the boy at sea were not forgotten. I learned to scrub the deck with holystone until the deck timbers shone in the sun. I learned to sand and paint the railings with neat's-foot oil[2] to preserve the wood, to polish the brass work and I did all of the other menial tasks which were required for the daily needs of life at sea. I was the Captain's son but that counted for little; for it was at his request that I was to be treated like all of the other young boys who sailed the many ships out of our home port. Eventually I grew in size and knowledge and earned the right to be rated as a Seaman. This was after father allowed me to go aloft and climb the shrouds[3] with the other young boys who were learning the ropes. The shrouds stretched down from the tops of each of the stepped masts. Between the shrouds of strong, tar-covered hemp were the thin ratlines[4] of finer rope. These were tarred also and often needed repair for they sometimes broke after years of naked feet and boots treading upon them. At first, our trips aloft were just training exercises – lessons to be learned before we could be trusted to join the other, experienced hands in working the sails. Most of us were under sixteen years of age and going aloft for the first time was a daunting experience.

---

[2] This is a yellow oil derived from the bones of cattle and is applied to the unpainted timber of a ship to preserve the wood from saltwater. The timber is first washed off with fresh water, dried and then the oil is applied lightly with a cloth.

[3] Shrouds are the standing rigging (permanent and fixed as opposed to the running rigging used to hoist sails etc.) which come down from the masts to the side of the ship holding them in place.

[4] Ratlines are a series of small rope lines fastened across a sailing ship's shrouds like the rungs of a ladder, used for climbing the rigging. Often made from thin rope or coarse twine and tarred, they frequently break and need replacement.

Hands aloft to furl the sails!

A full set of sails

4

"Hands aloft!" the First Mate, Mr Warren, would cry and we would run to the gunwales[5] to begin our long, slow climb.

Up we would climb to the maintop; that small platform which was near the top of the main mast where the shrouds narrowed to nothing before spreading out again back outwards to the edge of the top. These were the futtock shrouds[6]; my first cause for fear about the ship. To climb them, one has to lean out backwards and climb upside down over the swaying deck forty feet[7] below. At first, I had a great fear of losing my grip and falling to the deck below, but in time I learned how to climb around the side of the futtocks to clamber up and over the edge of the top and on to the safety of that small, swaying platform. In some of the larger vessels, the main top had small openings cut into each side just above the futtock shrouds. These were the "lubber's holes" through which the inexperienced sailors or lubbers could climb without having to arch backwards and climb the futtock shrouds. Of course, had our maintop had such a convenience we would not use them. It was a matter of pride for us new boys to show that we were as good as any sailor.

---

[5] The top edge of the ship's side or bulwark.

[6] These are supporting shrouds which run from the outer edges of a top downwards and inwards to a point on the mast or lower shrouds, and carry the load of the shrouds that rise from the edge of the top.

[7] Forty feet is about 12 metres as one foot is about 30 centimetres

Here the lower mast was joined to the topmast which was dovetailed and bolted on to and around the spindle of the mast below. The whole of this joint is bound by iron bands, and between the bands, by rope firmly turned around, and nailed tight. Three shrouds and their ratlines extended up the top mast to the cross-trees which were mere spars extending only a short distance out from its top. The topmast was similarly joined to the topgallant mast above it - the final vertical part of the rigging. Two more shrouds on each side went to the top of this mast which finally terminated in the flagstaff.

One day, after we had been thoroughly trained in the 'up-and-over' exercise, that is, climbing up to the maintop and then down the ratlines on the other side to the deck; one of my contemporaries dared me to 'kiss the jack'. This was usually reserved as a punishment meted out to young midshipmen – trainee officer – on board Navy ships. The defaulter would have to climb to the very top of the topgallant mast[8], then shimmy up the flagstaff and kiss the 'jack' or flat cap at its top. In many of the larger ships, this could leave the youngster trembling at well over 120 feet above the deck. Our small ship did not rate a mainmast[9] quite as high, but it still was a frightening prospect. Naturally I accepted out of bravado rather than common sense. Perhaps it was because I was the son of the captain

---

[8] Topgallant masts are often the tallest mast, being above the topmast which is above the lower mast.

[9] Mainmast is often the central and most important mast of a three-masted vessel. The front mast is the foremast and that at the stern is the mizzenmast.

or perhaps it was an act of stubbornness. So I climbed. Up the shrouds to the main top I went and then around the dreaded futtock shrouds. Having reached the maintop, I then had to climb the narrow shrouds and ratlines of the topmast and topgallant mast. Having reached the bottom of the flagstaff, I grasped it with both arms and legs and slowly pushed myself to the jack on top. Having completed my task, I returned slowly to the deck, sliding hand-over-hand down the starboard backstay which joined the mast just below the maintop to the gunwale of the ship.
Our next lesson aloft was more dramatic and for that, better training although we did not think so at the time.

"All 'ands aloft ta furl sail!" called the first mate; and he meant 'all hands'! Even us trainees who had only just mastered the fear of climbing the mainmast to the maintop and then the upside-down scramble over the dreaded futtock shrouds. Our gallant little ship[10] –for she was fully rigged, even on our mizzenmast – had just gone about to run before a fresh gale which had suddenly sprung up from the southeast. To add to our misery there was a strong swell running from the south due to the previous direction of the Northwest Trades – giving a 'confused swell', according to the first mate who took such conditions as a matter of course. To our inexperienced eyes, the sea and our little ship were in great turmoil with the only confusion being in our own terrified minds. This was our first lesson in furling

---

[10] A vessel rigged with three masts with square-rigged (sails across the vessel) on all three masts and a fore-and-aft sail called a 'spanker' on the rear or mizzenmast.

or stowing a sail by edging out along the narrow footropes slung beneath the yards – those rounded wooden spars to which the tops of the sails were attached and which usually ran out at right-angles to the masts. Getting onto the yard was easy. One had to step down from the maintop onto the bunt – that first short section of the yard closest to the mast – and around the slings of metal rope which held it to the mast. The next manoeuvre was the most difficult part. This required one to ease down onto the narrow and very flexible footropes that were slung several feet below the yard itself. These were made from a strong hemp less than an inch in diameter which freely swung with every movement of the body. Placing the first foot upon the rope caused a very uneasy feeling of insecurity for it swung to and fro with great rapidity. There was an unwritten rule about going out on a yard, in fact climbing anything; three points of contact meaning two hands and a foot or two feet and a hand. For the first time going onto a yard, one needed every point of contact which the body would allow. On top of the yard itself was the jackstay[11], a stiff length of rope which ran along the entire length of the yard. This was then attached to the top of the canvas sail. In some larger ships, this jackstay was often a long steel rod attached at several points to the wooden yard by metal slings. This was my first and only lifeline and I grasped it with the eagerness of fear before venturing my second foot on the rope below. Having clung to the yard and its jackstay and with both feet

---

[11] Jackstay - is a safety bar running along a ship's yard.

now on the footropes, I edged out along the yard. First, I would move a foot along the swinging rope below and then I would move my grasp further long the jackstay. Mercifully I was the fourth hand out on the yard and so only had to move a few feet clear of the maintop. Once in my position, I clung with great determination to the jackstay rope, my body arching only partly over the yard and the stiff canvas which was tightly curved outwards from the front of the yard. There was no grip onto this canvas yet. Below the yard my legs, bent slightly at the knees, swung back and forth as though my body was having convulsions. This did not help my stability and so I gripped the jackstay with all of my strength wondering how I was going to work on the sail.

"Lock ya legs, matey!" came a cry from the outward gloom of the yard, for it was almost nightfall and a slight drizzle had fallen upon the vessel.

I straightened my legs and found to my joy that my convulsive oscillations stopped and the rope below seemed to feel much firmer. I was able now to lean up and further over the yard from my waist upwards and this gave me even greater stability and my grasp on the jackstays relaxed.

Below I heard the first mate call through his speaking trumpet "Let go sheets[12], haul away on tha' lines!"

---

[12] Sheets are lines attached to sails and are used to control their position.

By these commands, the two watches remaining on deck undid the sheets which were the ropes which had been used to haul the sails down and then fastened them around belaying pins held in holes on the pinrails[13] on the inside edges of the bulwarks or around the bottoms of the masts. The excess lengths of these sheets had been neatly coiled upon the deck or flaked in long, parallel lines so that the sheets would fly freely once the command of "Haul aft!" was given.

By these actions the canvas sails were hauled up to their respective yards. There, the crew aloft had to grasp the canvas – always stiff and wet and sometimes covered with ice from the cold spray. Having folded and tucked the canvas along the yards, small lengths of rope called gaskets were then tied around the sail and back onto the jackstay on the top of the yard. Having taken in the sails, the crew then climbed down the shrouds if new to the game or slid quickly to the deck hand-over-hand down a convenient backstay[14].

And so, my education aboard a whaler progressed. In time I learned the complicated art of navigation, taking a fix with the sextant and plotting courses upon the chart. Eventually I was trusted with command of one of the whalers – the small open boats which chased the whale across the sea.

---

[13] Pinrails are a rack that holds belaying pins to which sheets and other lines can be secured and are placed along the bulwarks (sides) or around the base of a mast.
[14] Part of the standing rigging supporting the mast which runs from the mast back along the side of the ship

These had a crew of five oarsmen, the tiller captain and the harpooner who stood at the bow ready to plunge one of many lances which were kept in a special caddy at the bow. Having been thrown, the rope attached to the end of harpoon would quickly leap out of its tub to follow our prey. After an appropriate time, the harpooner would quickly and expertly secure the line around the wooden bollard right at the boat's bow. Then we were off! Our sailormen called it a 'Nantucket Sleigh Ride' for our little boat would suddenly jump and skim across the water attached to the great beast on the other end of the line. It took all of my strength to hold the tiller straight so that the boat would run smoothly through the waves and not turn and capsize as the great whale turned every which way in order to remove the great lance in its back. Often the whale would dive and our line would be loosened or even thrown into the sea, but then she would broach, coming to the surface with a great splash and wallow of its great body. More harpoons from the other boats would strike home until the great whale finally gave up and died. Now the thrill of the chase and the excitement of our manoeuvres were replaced by a great sorrow for the poor beast which we had killed. At least that was my feeling, but for some it was just another successful whale kill and if we were lucky, there would be no injuries to the crew nor damage to the boats.

I grew into manhood and passed all requirements of the Marine Board to be Master of a sea-going vessel. My father was very proud of this but he had some reservations about my ability to lead men. I too, had my doubts. I had mastered most of the skills required by those handling a vessel at sea: I could steer by the stars and navigate by chart and compass and I could handle the sails as well as any man aloft or on deck. I was, however never comfortable going aloft nor was I excited at steering a small boat when chasing the whale. Nor was I completely at home in the company of carousing sailormen, either at sea in their foc'sle[15] nor on land in the many taverns and inns which clustered around the waterfront.

---

[15] foc'sle is an abbreviation of forecastle, the accommodation area in the bow or fore part of the ship usually reserved for the crew.

Chapter Two
Saved from the Ice

Latitude: 63°44′49″ North; Longitude: 68°31′02″ West
8⁰F, winds mainly Northwest at 10 knots

When I was in my twentieth year, my father sent me on a cruise into the North Atlantic as third mate aboard the *Norfolk Lass*, captained by my father's good friend Captain Amos Shilling. A few weeks after we sailed, father took his ship, the *Aquinnah*[1] north along the coast and into the Labrador Sea. Here, west of Greenland, he hoped to find new waters in which to hunt for whales as they migrated south in October after feeding in the high latitude. He had specifically asked me to go with Captain Amos at this time and not go with him in his command. At the time I thought nothing of this for Captain Amos was an old hand at whaling and father said that I needed his experience. Perhaps he knew of the dangers of his voyage and did not want me on board his ship.

When I returned from our venture into the mid-Atlantic, I found the people of New Bedford in a great state of unhappiness and sorrow. Tying up at our place at the quay was not the usual joyous homecoming. There was a solemn air of foreboding. My mother was at the quay, as well as

---

[1] The name comes from Aquinnah, once called Gay Head, a town located on the island of Martha's Vineyard in Massachusetts. It is the area inhabited by the native Wampanoag people and means "land under the hill."

many of the womenfolk of our crew and we all knew that something was amiss.

My father's ship had not returned. It had been many months since they had left and it was many more until word had come by way of a Canadian trading ship that the crew were at the Inuit[2] village at Frobisher Bay[3]. Captain Amos immediately made the *Norfolk Lass* ready for sea and there were many eager volunteers to go to sea. I went as second mate and we sailed the next day. It was over thirteen hundred nautical miles to this remote Inuit settlement and we all hoped that the sea ice had cleared from its long inlet.

There was fog at the start of our journey which did not bode well so we tacked[4] slowly southwest down Buzzard's Bay, then turned due east to clear Nantucket Island to take advantage of the prevailing sou' westerlies and the edge of the Gulf Stream current flowing north. Once well clear of our beloved continent, our course was a straight heading to the northeast and a long one of over 800 nautical miles into the Labrador Sea. Here we turned to the north west and headed on to Frobisher Bay. We had good luck and good sailing. For the most part we ran before a fair wind and at

---

[2] Inuit (meaning the people) are the members of one of the indigenous peoples of northern Canada, parts of Greenland and Alaska. Often the term 'Eskimo' has been used by Europeans but this often is considered unacceptable by the Inuit and Yupik peoples.
[3] This is in the Canadian territory of Nunavut and since 1987 it has been called Iqaluit.
[4] Tacking is a manoeuvre by which a sailing vessel, whose desired course is into the wind, turns its bow toward the wind so that the direction from which the wind blows changes from one side to the other, allowing progress in the desired direction.

times our log[5] showed eight knots[6]. The sea was relatively free of any ice, with just a few rough-topped growlers at first and then many more smaller floes of old ice. We kept an extra watch at all times and sailed with reduced sail at night with only our fore-and-aft sails rigged. It was a fast passage and on the morning of the tenth day we sighted the low, snow-covered rolling hills of the settlement.

Perhaps the term settlement was too grand a term; for it consists of only a few houses, mostly small huts made of piles of stone covered with driftwood and skins. Here and there were some raised frameworks of driftwood for drying fish for this was the specific occupation of this encampment. Captain Amos, who was a learned man, explained to me that the Inuit people on this south eastern side of Baffin Island were the descendants of the Thule people who called this place Iqaluit, meaning place of fish.

We anchored the *Norfolk Lass* in the bay and all hands except for a small anchor watch launched the whale boats and rowed to the shore. A large group of Inuit had gathered on the stony beach with some of the survivors of the *Aquinnah* to welcome us. All were clad in a variety of furs and headwear, the round, friendly faces of the Inuit were a welcoming sight after many days of apprehension at sea.

---

[5] A ship's casting line or log (as opposed to a written journal of the same name) was a circular float attached to a long, light line which had knots tied into it at certain intervals. To find the speed of the ship, the log was thrown overboard and the number of knots passing through the hand during the passage of sand in a half-minute "hourglass" was noted.

[6] A Knot is one nautical mile (1.1508 miles or 1,852 metres or one minute of latitude along the Equator) per hour.

Most of the Inuit spoke some English and soon small groups were leading members of our crew off to where their friends or relatives were housed. Those survivors who were on the beach were heartily embraced by all.

Jacob Wishing, the third mate of the *Norfolk Lass* came to me, pointing to a family of Inuit who stood a little distance from the beach.

"Mr. Jamie, sir! Your father has been lodged with this family. They wish to take you to him."

"Thank'ee, Mr. Wishing. That is most kind of you." I hurried after the family who had turned and were heading up the beach to the huts. Not far from the beach, and located on a small rise was a small house made from timber. It was bigger than most, well-constructed with a roof of cut shingles. The head of the family, a tall man with a broad frame and open, friendly face bade me enter. His name I learned later was Ipirvik and he was both the leader of this small community and the local angakkuq or shaman[7] of these people.

Sitting on a bed across the room was my father. He was attempting to rise but Ipirvik rushed over and gently helped him to stand. With Ipirvik's help he hobbled over to me and embraced me sobbing.

"My son, my son! I had thought that I would never see you again."

---

[7] Someone who is regarded as having access to, and influence in, the world of benevolent and malevolent spirits and practices divination and healing.

"It is alright, now father." I replied, helping him back to his bed. "You are safe now and Captain Amos has come to take you all home."

"Joy to you, my boy. I will be alright now. Go and help Amos with our people for many of them need more care than I."

"Him good, now," said Ipirvik who put his arm around my shoulder and led me out of the house. "My wife, Tookuluk care for him good."

Indeed, these kind, generous people had rescued the crew of the *Aquinnah* several months ago and had taken the survivors into their homes and shared whatever they had, as is their custom, for their care and restoration. Those of Captain Amos' crew who were not taken into the family homes which housed the survivors, were taken to the warm village hall where they were made comfortable. After visiting the survivors as was my father's wish, I returned to Ipirvik's house where I was given a small cot near my father.

We stayed with the people of Iqaluit for several weeks whilst some of the weaker members of the survivors gained more strength, although all were eager to go aboard the *Norfolk Lass* and return home. Those who were fit enough continued to help their Inuit hosts with any of the menial chores which daily living in this extreme climate demanded. Eventually the story of the rescue of the crew of the *Aquinnah* became known, for it had become a well-spoken story which would be told for many years by these generous and happy people.

The *Aquinnah* had sailed further to the west that my father had anticipated due to the fact that the ship's compass pointed more in this direction than true north. This occurred because at these high latitudes, Magnetic North was more west than actual north, being located somewhere in northern Canada than at the Geographical North Pole. Also, there had been a sudden inset of cold weather and having taken shelter in a small inlet on the south eastern shores of Baffin Island, the sea had frozen, trapping the *Aquinnah* in the ice. With some thawing and the motion of the sea currents in the bay, the barque[8] was slowly crushed by the moving ice. My father had landed as many stores as possible on the shores of the bay but traversing the moving ice pack was done only with some difficulty using the ship's small jolly boat which was the only boat which could be manoeuvred between the ice floes. Having got all of the men ashore and made a simple shelter of rocks and canvas, father could only watch as his vessel broke up and eventually disappeared between the raised blocks of moving ice.

With their ship sunk beneath the ice, the crew of the *Aquinnah* had no option but to head south in an attempt to find human habitation in the bleak north of Canada. Father

---

[8] A sailing ship, typically with three masts, in which the foremast and mainmast are square-rigged and the mizzenmast is rigged fore and aft.

had had his men fit out the small jolly boat[9], which they had removed before the barque was crushed, as a sled; the larger whale boats being difficult to manage across the ice. This they loaded with the meagre stores which they had saved and two of the men who had been injured from falling spars and several others who were suffering from exposure. The crew then dragged the small boat across the ice of the bay and then up into the snow-covered hills, always heading south. The small boat compass was of course unreliable this far north, so they relied on a makeshift sun compass, a form of hand-held sundial constructed out of timber by their Norwegian carpenter, Lars. This compass consisted of a small round disk through which was passed a long, vertical stick at right-angles to the plane of the disk. He had learned this art from his grandfather who often told him tales of how the vikvær[10] sailed across the North Sea to Greenland. They too used a sun compass in the dim twilight of the north and sólarsteinn[11] or sun stones, to find the sun when it was hidden by fog. The Captain had estimated the direction of Geographical North from the short passage of the sun and Lars had marked the position of its highest shadow on the disk of his sun compass. He also marked the sun's shadows at different times before and after noon so that they could

____

[9] A small ship's boat, typically hoisted at the stern of the ship and used for general purposes such as ferrying small parties ashore.
[10] These were people from Viken, the historical name for part of south-eastern Norway, but could be applied to Vikings in general from any of the Scandinavian ports.
[11] Sólarsteinn or sun stones were transparent crystals of calcite mineral called Iceland Spar which could polarise light when rotated to show the position of the sun in fog or even when it went below the horizon.

Whale Ho!

Aquinnah trapped in the ice

find the direction south at given times of the day. Unfortunately, they did not have the Iceland Spar crystals necessary as sun stones when they encountered fog. So, my father and his crew pressed on across the icy wastes of Baffin Island (so they rightly believed). At night they sheltered against the side of the boat with a makeshift tent of canvas and the flames of two small whale oil lamps. The two of the injured men died from their injuries and two more from the life-sapping cold. My father, who had given the fur lining of his sea boots to a sailor who had briefly fallen through the ice, insisted on taking his turn on the haul ropes and had suffered badly from the cold with his toes eventually becoming gangrenous.

It was more by good luck than their skills of navigation that after many days of hard endurance they had encountered a hunting party from the Frobisher Bay settlement. The Inuit were most distressed at the survivors' condition and constructed snow shelters and used furs to give them more comfort. They shared their food with them and sent runners back to the settlement for help. Within a few days the entire crew had been carried back to the settlement on sleds and given care for their exposure to the cold. It was in this condition that we had found the survivors of the *Aquinnah* at Frobisher Bay.

Chapter Three
The Land of the Vikings

Latitude 60° 23' 49" North; Longitude 5° 19' 28" East.
62⁰F, winds mainly Northwest at 8 knots

It has been almost two years now since my father and his crew had been rescued. No-one here at New Bedford thought ill of my father; it was the way of the seaman's world to suffer at sea, especially in that bleak wilderness of rock, ice and water off Baffin Island to the north.

The Captain however could not forgive himself for leading his men in such a disastrous voyage and he constantly cursed himself for being so foolish as to have gone off course and to be trapped in the ice. My mother Elaine, always seemed to have the strength to overcome most setbacks and gently chided my father at these times and tried to give him what comfort she could. She was a remarkable woman; perhaps she needed to be for marrying my father and surviving those long months whilst he was at sea hunting the great whale. There was the house to manage and my sisters and I as well as the business end of father's whaling enterprises. She did all of this with calm, efficiency and always a smile when she needed to solve one of our many childhood problems or in dealing with the complexities and people involved in the whaling industry in the town.

The Captain had taken to his study of late and showed a considerable amount of agitation. There were many times when he would call for our carriage and go into town without a word to mother or any of us in the house. There was also a constant stream of telegrams being brought to our door by Roger the local Telegraph Boy on his old pony. Father had regained much of his old self again, but he occasionally fell to melancholy when he remembered his last voyage. When he returned home, our doctor had amputated several of father's toes on one foot and most of the other which had become gangrenous. So now he was forced to use a stick when he walked; a great disgrace in his way of thinking. He had always had a generous heart to those old seamen who had lost a limb to the whale or other accident of their trade, but he could not reconcile himself as being a cripple.

Lately however, some of his old confidence had returned and he hinted that good things were yet to be revealed and so he bustled around the house and locked himself in his study. I went with him at times into the town where he would leave me at our favourite venue, the Wamsutta Club on Orchard Street whilst he 'did business' as he called it, elsewhere in the town. He would always return a short time later, mostly without a word, we would have a light lunch and then return up the hill in our carriage. One day, I remember it well for it was raining and there was a cold wind blowing in from the north, father returned from his usual business trip with a telegram in his hand and a very satisfied smile on his face.

"At last! At last! All the arrangements have been made!" he said as he sat down at our table. "We have a new vessel!" he said with a fire in his eye which I had not seen for many a year.

He passed the telegram over to me; *'Your ship is finished and ready for you. Andersen.'* It simply read, but who was this person Andersen?

Father looked at me for a while and retrieved the letter. "I will tell you now, but nary a word to your mother just yet. There are still some final details to attend to." He said in a quiet voice as though mother was in this very room.
"I have not only been a grumpy old invalid these last two years," he said with a slight twinkle in his eye. "I have been building a new ship – or at least Peder Andersen has been building our new ship; in Bergen, Norway. Or so he calls it. But it is still part of the Kingdom of Sweden so he should be called a Swede, think you not?" He said in a sharp, excited way.

"But father," I exclaimed. "We all thought that you had done with the sea!"

"Oh, aye. That's what many thought of poor Abraham Toby, but it's difficult to wash the sea entirely out of the blood. My days of pacing the deck and taking the tiller of a whaleboat are indeed gone, but I cannot lose the need to hunt the whale. It's in our family nature, you see?" he said with some passion.

He quickly brushed all things off his large, wooden desk and unrolled a huge chart. On it were the detailed plans of a ship, the likes of which. It was, to be sure a sailing vessel; ship rigged, that is to say it had all three masts square-rigged. It also had a tall, thin smoke stack or chimney just forward of the mizzen mast.

"An auxiliary steamer!" I exclaimed.

"Yes, my boy." Father answered with enthusiasm. "And with many things that a whalerman would love to have but are only to be found in some of the larger packet ships. Let me tell you about her."

Father moved around the desk and sat down in the large armchair which he kept in the study for relaxation. He too his pipe down from the rack in the corner, filled it from the old jar on the desk and struck his match on the sole of his shoe.

"She's a steam-powered ship as you can see. We have no name for her yet, but that will come soon. I have had her built in Bergen in Norway because they build good ships and know about the sea and ice.

Peder Andersen is a good man. I met him once in Christiania when I was there on business. He apprenticed under that remarkable shipwright Colin Archer of Larvik. Now don't be fooled by that English name." he said, pointing the stem of his pipe in my direction. "He's as

Norwegian as the Fjords but had a Scotch father and was born in Larvik itself. Andersen is very much the master shipwright in Bergen now. He runs a tight yard, he does; won't employ any shipwright or worker who hasn't served on a whaler or sealer. He reckons that men must know how to use his ships as well as how to make 'em. His men know what it's like to tread an icy deck with the sleet a-blowin' in their faces. Aye, and he knows about ice as well. Many of his men have sailed from their home shores out into those cold, tempestuous waters of the North Atlantic. – what they called the Norwegian Sea – across to Iceland and even beyond to Greenland in search of the whale or the seal. Aye, a good man is Peder Andersen who is building our new ship."

Father got up from his chair – with some difficulty I noted – and moved around the desk. He spread the roll out again and fastened its edges with the few heavy objects remaining on the desk.

"Look ye!" he motioned with the stem of his pipe. "Two hundred and ten feet long! Why, we were lucky to build one over one hundred feet in the old days. And she has a beam of nearly thirty feet! That'll make her a good sea boat, it will."

By now father was in a great mood. The old gleam was back in his eye; I have seen it at sea when we have sighted a whole pod of great whales and he yelled "all boats away" and the hunt began.

"She is indeed a wonderful ship, father." I said "But I have seen similar designs of auxiliary steamers proposed in the popular press. The Scots of Dundee have started making small paddle steamers and they have been very successful off their shores."

"Not like this 'un!" he said sharply. "It may look similar to these little fancy ships, but this vessel is something entirely different. Those new Scotch ships may go to sea and even into the ice, but they won't last. Some are remarkably strong ships but I wager that they will be crushed in any ice pack just like the poor old *Aquinnah*. No! My ship is different. Strong, yes. Andersen has built her out of oak, with the main joints and braces made from shapes naturally grown, not cut. She has a double hull on oak ribs closely spaced – here, look at these dimensions!" he motioned to some of the fine numbers which ranged around the main drawing of the ship's construction. "All the joints and placement timbers have been cross-braced and bolted, not nailed and she's clad in thick timbers of greenheart. Do ye know what that is boy?" he said, raising his face to look at me. Without waiting for an answer, for he knew that I was ignorant of the term, he continued.

"It's a hardwood from the forests of South America. Andersen and some of the other Norwegians have it specially imported. It is a remarkable wood. Almost too hard to work with the usual tools, it is both strong and resistant without being too brittle. It will flex with the rest of the ship in a good sea and it resists the sharp teeth of any ice flow."

I was suitably impressed by these details. It certainly would be a strong ship. "But strong ships have still been crushed in the ice." I answered.

"Not this one!" my father laughed. "Andersen is also a clever naval architect as well as one of the greatest shipwrights. It is the shape of the hull that has been the downfall of all of those other ships, no matter how strong they be, the moving ice is always stronger. Our ship has been built in a special way. Not only will it be able to push through the ice pack like those others, but when it gets locked in and the ice squeezed like a vice, our ship will simply rise up above those dreadful jaws."

My puzzled look only added to father's enthusiasm. He was once more the experienced sea captain explaining some sea skill to his apprentice. "Across its wide beam, its hull would look in cross-section to have a soft double chine[1]. You understand?"

---

[1] In boating, this refers to a sharp change in angle in the cross section of a ship's hull. A hull without chines has a gradually curving cross section whereas a soft chine as with the hull as described here would still involve the meeting of distinct planes but be more rounded at base.

I nodded agreement, not seeing how the side of a ship which has a double chine, that is sides with slightly different angles. Father continued:

"Well, perhaps chine might be too severe a term, because the hull angle does change, not sharply also like an S-shaped cross-section but flatter – almost rounded like a bowl at base but getting suddenly steeper higher up, like. Andersen reckons that when the ice pushes in, it will come up against the lower sides of the ship at such a low angle that it will push the whole ship upwards rather than inwards. Our great ship will rise up on top of the ice and not be crushed by it. When the thaw comes, she will gently slip back into the water. What say ye now, boy?"

"That is remarkable father. I said. "But a vessel this size will take a fair wind to even move it through the most open of oceans."

"That is to be sure." said he. "But she has three strong masts of Baltic pine and a huge sail area for its size. Moreover, when the winds fail us, or the ice pack becomes heavy, we will have our own power. One hundred and sixty horses will pull us with our new steam engine. Think of it! All of this power to push our craft through the ice. And if we get stuck, we simply pull in our screw like a turtle pulls in its head - and our rudder too – so they will not be broken and then drop them down again in clear water."

"She will need to carry a lot of coal then." I answered.
Father looked concerned and tapped the plan with his pipe.
"Indeed, it will son. But that is another one of Andersen's
clever plans. We will have a good amount of space below
decks. More than any of the larger whalers that you have
sailed in and we will have two great freshwater tanks for
our reciprocating steam engine. One of them will also
double as an extra coal bunker once we have emptied it and
we can fill it from our last port of call. Thereafter, once we
have reached the ice there will be plenty of fresh water just
floating around us as ice."

"There will be plenty of room for the crew below decks."
He continued. "It'll take only a small crew for such a large
ship – no more than thirty men, including our two
engineers and their three stokers who shovel the coal. You
will be its First Mate and old Caleb Warren will be your
Second. The sails can be worked well from the deck – unless
they be furled[2], you understand – and the top'sls have been
split too, to reduce the deck handling."

That is a truly well-conceived design, sir." I replied as my
father rolled up the chart. "When shall we be able to see
her?"

"Soon, lad. I have convinced Captain Shilling that he
should make a small deviation when he puts to sea in the

---

[2] Sails are furled when they have been hauled up to the yardarms and then tied with
gaskets – small lengths of rope which hold the folded sails onto the top of the yardarm.

Norfolk Lass. Bergen is just a short way up the Norwegian coast and just east of his desired whaling area. We will take only a reduced crew and our engineers of course, and go to Andersen's yard early next month. I want you to come too, so make no more commitments here."

True to his word, Captain Amos Shilling made arrangements for our reduced crew to come onboard the *Norfolk Lass* on the first of the month and we sailed two days later. Our passage was swift as we ran before a stiff sou'wester and in eight days we were just north of the Orkneys. Here, we veered east and came upon the rugged Norwegian coastline just as the sun was setting. We hove to for the night and then continued our journey next morning south along Store Sotra, the large island which is due west of Bergen. At its southern tip, we again turned northeast, taking a wide berth around the island of Viksøyna and headed up the wide channel north of Store Kalsøy. Here we sailed into the Fanafjorden, the long inlet leading to the village of Fanahammeren, just nine miles south of Bergen.

Captain Shilling anchored here for the night and in the morning father and I and our small crew went ashore. We had telegraphed the Andersen Yard from home before our departure and so we found several wagons waiting for us and in a few hours we were in the centre of Bergen. The Captain – for now my father had assumed his rightful place as the captain of our new ship – Mr Dunsmuir the Engineer and I as First Mate and Mr Warren our Second Mate, found our rooms already booked at the elegant Hotel Splendid overlooking the Fish Markets at the end of the Bergen Havn, the long inlet which is the main entrance port of the city's centre. The rest of our small crew had been given rooms in the Seaman's Mission not far from the inlet.

The next morning father and I were breakfasting in the large dining room of the hotel when we were approached by a well-dressed man.

"Captain Tobey, it is good to see you again" he said, extending his hand in friendship.

When my father stood up, the man continued. "Please forgive this early morning interruption to your breakfast but it was a nice day for a walk and I thought that we should now meet. Remember me? I am Peder Andersen."

My father eagerly shook the man's outstretched hand and smiled. "Well so it is a good morning, Mister Andersen. A pleasure to meet you! Please, sit and have some coffee with us won't you? This is my son, James." Father said as he motioned to me.

"Good morning James Tobey, it is nice to meet you also." He said with abroad smile. "Thank you, I will be happy to have a cup with you. Jostein Halvorsen serves a good cup here. You like his hotel, yes?"

"Yes, thank you." Father replied. "The rooms are very comfortable and I have no doubt that the service, like his coffee will also be good."

"Ah, that is nice. Thank you" Andersen said with a smile. He was perhaps a little older than father, short but stocky and his round face was tanned and creased with the many wrinkles that only years at sea could make. What was striking about his features were his thick grey hair and his clear blue eyes which lit up when he smiled; which he did often in a natural, open manner. His manner of speaking, though soft was very animated and full of enthusiasm. I felt that Andersen was a man who was happy with life and could be trusted when things became sour. Even then, his smile would beam through. I often later saw him in his shipyard taking to his men and apprentices. When something adverse happened within the yard he would simply pat the offender on the back and smiling would say "Ah that is good value in extra training for you!" Few things seemed to worry this man who always seemed to have a solution for most problems.

For now, he leaned across the table with a concerned look on his face. "I am sorry to tell you, Captain Tobey, but it will be a few more days until your ship will be ready."

Father had already gauged the nature of our new friend for he had become an astute judge of character during his many years at sea. "Well now, Mister Andersen, that should not be too much of a worry to us. After all, it has been over a year since our first communications and we Yankees don't mind waiting a little while more for a good outcome."

"Thank you, Captain. My men have built your ship with loving care to all of your specifications and we are proud of her. You wait! It will surprise you for she is a thing of beauty. But alas, our modern innovation is the delay. Alas, the steam engine supplied by my good friend Erik Sørensen took a little longer to arrive from Christiania[3] and his men are just now doing the final tests. Perhaps a few days more if you please." Andersen spread his hands out at this last comment.

"Well, that was not in your control, so do not worry about it. It will give us time to look around your beautiful town. We were too exhausted last night to have a good look at it for all we wanted was a good room and a soft bed. And I might add that your Mister Halvorsen has provided us with both and an excellent breakfast as well!"

"Ah, that is good, then." Andersen beamed" but please call me Peder. We Norwegians are a democratic lot and do not use honorifics too often. 'Peder Andersen' is about as formal as I get called and my men call me 'den Gamle Mannen' or 'the Old Man' – behind my back, you understand. We have a good life at the yard and build ships with love. Then let us say the end of the week to meet at my yard. You can show your son around our city. We are very proud of it. It is a good place to come back to from the sea even when there is ice on the water." He laughed.

---

[3] Now renamed Oslo

With that, he stood up and with his infectious smile gave us a slight bow. "Until then, Family Tobey, ha det! - or 'good bye' as you would say!"

"Well, now!" Father said. "That was a fine meeting. He seems a good man, Andersen. He has pride in what he does without the need to windbag it. Good! We will finish our breakfast and, if you do not mind, I will ask you to walk along the quay to the Seamen's Mission and tell our crew what is happening and that Friday is our day. You may give them some little advance in their wages but warn them that they are the guests of these fine people and so their behaviour must be what we expect at home. No heavy drinking! They use the Kroner here as currency so stop into the bank across the way and exchange our Yankee dollars. I know that most people hereabouts speak reasonable English. Now off you go, Jamie and I will see you back here shortly."

The use of my Christian name was a good start. Father only ever used it when he was in the best of moods. I left the hotel and crossed the cobbled square. It was paved in large, smooth rectangular stones which seemed to spread out to the buildings across the way. These were very presentable. Not the uniform grey edifices which I had seen in some of the big cities in my own country. Each had its own character; some were of only two stories and others went to four or five. Their colours varied, too. White, cream and light brown seemed to be the most popular colours, but here and there were buildings pained red or blue or yellow. All were neat and tidy with steeply sloping, tiled rooves.

Some buildings, especially along the narrow lanes which led away from the square, had a flag hanging over their doorway. This flag was indeed colourful, having a red background behind a blue cross edged in white lying on its side. In the top inside corner was a more complex design having triangular segments and a small cross of white, blue and yellow. After I had made our transactions at the bank, I enquired about this flag which hung above the bank's front door. The teller, who like many people here spoke excellent English, laughed"

"Oh ja! That is our flag. We call it the 'Sildesalaten', which in English is the 'salad of the herring, Ja? We call it that. With no disrespect, you know, because it looks like a plate of food on the table in which we have in both our Norway and also Sweden to which we are united. Who knows! Perhaps one day we will get our freedom and remove the salad from our flag!" He said with a broad grin.

I exchanged our dollars for the local currency and walked back across the cobbled square to the hotel. It was a bright sunny morning and a fresh wind was blowing down the inlet. It was warm for June and not much different from a day in New Bedford at this time of year. When I returned to the Hotel, I found father in the foyer talking to the proprietor, Mister Halvorsen. With him was a young man with that fairness of hair and complexion typical of many Scandinavian people. Father turned to greet me.

"Ah, Jamie. It is good that you are back. How was the banking?"

"All is well, Father. With your permission, I will take the men their wages and be back presently."

"Good. Please do so for I am arranging with Mister Halvorsen the use of his son, here and his carriage for a day's outing."

It was only a short walk along the sidewalk which followed the road running along the docks on the opposite side of the inlet from our hotel. A signpost in Norse told me that this place was called the Bryggen which I later found to mean the dock. Here were all manner of smaller craft; some coastal traders gaff rigged; smaller fishing vessels with one or two masts and several small steam-powered pinnaces[4]. The buildings along the dock were tidy and very business-like. Most were of wood, usually two or three stories high, brightly painted in many shades of reds, yellows and browns, with an occasional white. Their rooves were very steep and most had a ground-floor shop front which seemed to deal with either the shipping trade or other type of commercial activity for Bergen is a centre of this country's fishing industry. Father later told me that this long row of houses, cluster tightly together for protection against the winter's cold, are called the Hanseatic Houses which had been set up in the fourteenth century by the German trading company, the Hanseatic League[5].

---

[4] A pinnace is a small, open boat often with a sail used for general ferry work from the main ship. Later these became powered by a small steam engine.
[5] This was a confederation of merchants from Germany and other states around the Baltic Sea. They dominated trade, especially between the twelfth and fifteenth centuries.

Further along the road I came upon a tall stone tower and other large buildings. I stopped to admire the old buildings and a stranger passing by stopped and explained in good English, as he could see by my dress that I was a foreigner, that this was the Rosenkranztårnet. This apparently was built in the sixteenth century as a protective fortification, although the stranger told me that parts of the old hall dated to several hundred years earlier. I thanked him for his kindness and continued on my way around the headland at the end of the inlet.

Here the Bryggen seemed to change into the Skuteviksbodene, or so the signpost intimated. It was another road which I followed around the headland until I saw a large wooden building right on the dock with a painted sign on its wall which announced that this was the 'Den Norske Sjoemannsmisjon'. I had picked up some of the terms of the Norwegian or Norsk language and was able to clearly sea that this was The Norwegian Seaman's Mission.

Inside, our crew had made themselves at home with the other sailors in residence and were glad to see me. They were even more glad when I counted out their individual wages and told them that they had leave until Friday when they should report to Andersen's yard which was further around the point at a place called Sandviken.

"Ja! I know that place." Said Lars our Norwegian carpenter, who had sailed with father on many a voyage and who had also sailed out of many ports, including Bergen in his youth. "I vill get tha men there. Don't you worry much about that, Mister Jamie."

"Thank you." I replied, being somewhat touched at the honorific which the carpenter had given me. "I will see you all bright and early on Friday, then." And with a goodbye wave of my hand left them in excited conversation as to how and where to spend their wages in a town which well-catered for seamen.

The walk back to the hotel was uneventful and full of the settled visions of this part of Bergen. Neat, brightly-coloured wooden houses nestled together along the waterfront and spread up into the hills beyond. The people I met along the way seemed to match their houses and many raised their caps with a cheerful "God Dag!"

At the hotel, I found father with the fair-haired young man standing next to a small horse-drawn trap. Father introduced the young man as Jørn Halvorsen, the son of our proprietor who was to be our guide on a sight-seeing tour of Bergen.

Without much ado, we climbed up into the back of the trap as Jørn Halvorsen flicked the reins. We were off to see Bergen! "Please to call me Jørn." Said our driver. "If that is permitted. We are a friendly people here."

Father lightly patted Jørn on his shoulder "Capital! My son, here is Jamie, and you can just call me 'Captain' – in a casual sort of way, you understand. We older Yankees can be a little too formal at times, but we mean well."

Bergen, Norway

Bergen Havn and the Rosenkranztårnet

We clattered over the cobbles and through pretty streets all lined with houses, again neat and brightly coloured and often with flowers hanging from pots below their windows. Here and there we saw the Norwegian flag hanging above a door and Jørn explained that the people here were very patriotic but sometimes wished that they could gain their freedom from the union with Sweden.

Out of the main part of town, we began a slow climb along a narrow dirt road which ran around the western side of the large hill which overlooked the city. After a while we eventually came to the summit of the hill where a large, flat area had been landscaped as a lookout. Behind this and away from the city was a large forest of tall pine trees.

"This is Fløyfjellet, the name of the mountain top here." Said Jørn. "It is almost four hundred metres above sea level and one can see the entire city and the Fjords beyond."

It was a magnificent view to be sure. Looking north we could see the broad expanse of the fjord extending around high wooded hills and terminating into the two main inlets on which the city had been built. Immediately below us was the Bergen Havn the main port and where our hotel could be seen on its western side. Along the docks on either side of this port were many ships; both small and large with one, two and three masts. Back from the centre of the city was a large lake fringed by parkland and many colourful, red rooved houses.

"That is a most beautiful view. Yes?" said Jørn. "But let me show you something else that belongs to our country."

With that he beckoned us to turn and follow him up the small open space and into the tall forest of dark green pine trees. The floor of this forest was mostly rock; rough, cracked and mostly covered with a thick carpet of dark green moss.

"You have heard of our trolls?" asked Jørn with an impish look on his face and with one eyebrow raised. "No? Well they are the giant people of our stories and legends. They live in these forests. They shun all light and live in caves or under bridges during the day. Even the smallest ray of the sun will turn them to stone. Look! Here is one!"

With that he went over to a large rock outcrop and placed his hand upon part of its surface. Sure enough, with only slight imagination one could see a small face looking out from the mossy rock. The face was slightly larger than normal and was slightly inclined. It had a broad, flat nose and its mouth was wide but the lips were narrow. Only one eye could be seen through the moss and it was closed. The whole effect was that of someone who was restfully sleeping. Of course, this was only in our imagination for the face was made by the projections and crevices in the shaded, moss-covered rock. Still, the effect was most startling and I could see how such stories could grow. I am not normally of a superstitious nature, but I would not like to come to this forest alone at night.

Back on the trap, Jørn took us down from the lookout and then turned south of the city. We travelled though well-tended countryside dotted with small farms and buildings painted red with steeply sloped rooves of grey slate and window frames painted in white. Well to the south we could see the mountains with their extensive covering of green. After a delicious lunch provided by the hotel, we returned to Bergen.

Early next morning we breakfasted with our Engineer, Mr. Dunsmuir, who spoke very little.

Soon Jørn Halvorsen arrived with the hotel trap so we climbed aboard to be taken to Peder Andersen's yard at Sandviken. As this was only a short distance we soon arrived in front of the large, double gates of the yard.

"Velkommen!" called the yard manager who took father, Mr. Dunsmuir and myself to Andersen's office where he was waiting for our arrival.

"God morgen! Gentlemen. Good Morning! Welcome to my yard. Come, you must be impatient to see your ship, Ja?" With that he turned and beckoned us to follow. Coming into a large shed lined with many benches, shelves and with ropes and pulleys hanging from the ceiling he walked over to one of the workers who was wearing trousers and a loose-fitting smock. Upon hearing our steps, the worker turned around. To my surprize I saw that the worker was a woman.

What a striking person she was! More of a girl than a mature woman, she must have been no more than eighteen

Our Troll in the rock above Bergen

Liv climbing the mainmast of the *Australis*

years of age. Of small height and a slim figure her face was her most striking feature. She was fair of skin and her hair was cut short. She looked at Peder Andersen and then at father and me with a broad smile.

"This is my daughter Liv, gentlemen, and as you can see, she is my assistant in this yard. She is almost as good as me." He said with a laugh and the same smiling face as that of his lovely daughter.

Father doffed his hat and replied "Good morning Miss Andersen."

I could only stand bolted to the spot. I had the feeling that my mouth was opened but nothing came out. I was speechless. She was the most beautiful young girl that I have ever seen. "Umm..hello, Miss Andersen." I finally stammered. "It is nice to meet you."

How inadequate I felt in the presence of this lovely girl who had a strong physical presence and confidence which was uncommon in all of the young women who I have met at home. On our tour of Andersen's yard, she explained so many technical details to father that I soon became lost in everything but her grace and beauty.

Coming out of the huge shed, we found ourselves in an area of small docks with several open workboats moored alongside a long wooden wharf.

"Now, here is what you have come to see!" Andersen exclaimed pointing out into the bay. Looking in the direction which he was indicating we saw the most beautiful ship.

My first impression was of a long, graceful vessel. She had a raked bow with a low bowsprit and flat stern. She had three tall masts and was indeed ship rigged. The foremast was slightly shorter than the mainmast and she was completely dressed with furled canvas.

Father was overjoyed. He clapped his hands together and did a little Yankee jig on the wharf. "She's a right royal beauty, Andersen and that's no mistake. Thank'ee." Andersen and his daughter beamed at this praise.

Father turned to me with a gleam in his eye. "There she be, son. The *Australis*! I had Mister Andersen here launch her before he sent his cable to us. I thought that it would save time."

"The *Australis*!" I replied, barely able to control my excitement. "Does that not mean 'South', father?" I enquired.

"Aye, it does. South! South is what she is called and south she will go! And as I feel that it will need a fitter man than I, you will be her captain. South! South to Antarctica!"

Chapter Four
The *Australis*

The following week was one of turmoil swirling with mixed emotions. There were the final preparations for sailing to be made; the inspection and familiarization of our small crew with their new ship and all of the formalities needed for the hand-over of Andersen's ship to father's company.

As we were rowed out to the ship, I had time to appreciate her beauty although I was somewhat distracted by the presence of Miss Andersen sitting by my side. The *Australis* was indeed ship-rigged with a full set of square-rigged sails. Her hull was painted black with a thin red strip around her sides flush with the deck. The figurehead was a beautiful young woman with her hand outstretched, pointing the way south.

She was heavily built and braced, with a strongly raked bow to work in any ice pack. The heavy timbers and steeply raked bow allowed it to be driven up onto the ice, where its weight would help to break through all but the thickest pack. Her double- chined hull, which looked somewhat quaint, like that of a swat rowing boat, would allow her to be pushed up out of the ice should she be frozen in the ice pack. There was a considerable space between the foremast and the mainmast; for she was a whaler that needed deck

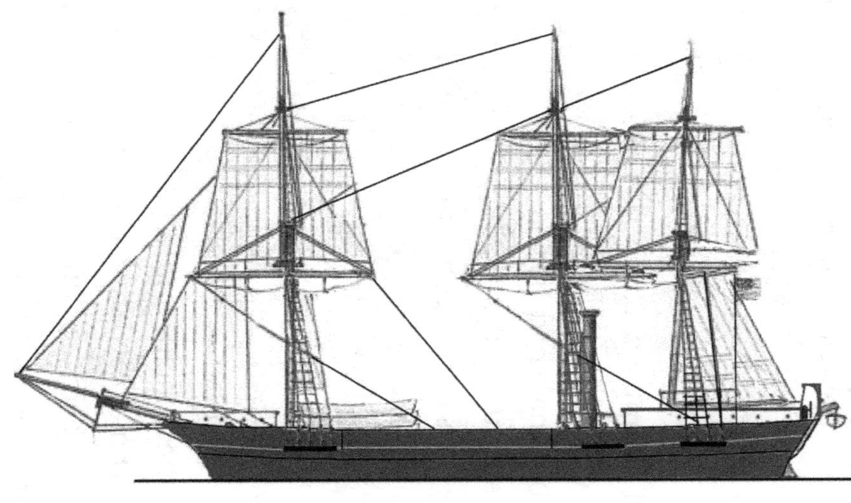

Australis

room for handling the processing of parts of the whales once they had been hauled on board.

It was though Peder Andersen was understanding my thoughts when he leaned over closer to father and said "You can see Captain Toby the vertical lines in the bulwarks between the two front masts, Ja? They are where you can lower that entire section of the bulwarks to be level with the deck. They are on hinges so the bulwarks can be dropped to lift the whale pieces easily on board."

Father nodded his approval for it was often difficult to haul massive parts of the whale on board once the flensing of cutting up of the whale had started. In the whaling trade at this time we still used the method known as outboard flensing. In the days of wooden sailing ships, there was not the means available to bring a dead whale on board to be processed or "flensed". So, the flensing took place by the side of the ship. This was known as outboard flensing. For this our new vessel had long timbers which would be run out from spaces just below the deck. The bulwarks would be lowered on their chains and supported by them and by these timbers. Thus, a wooden platform, or cutting stage would be formed, being slightly wider than the main deck amidships. The dead whale would be floated over to be secured to the side of the vessel below this extended deck. Holes would be cut into the whale's skin at various points to allow large wooden toggles to be inserted. Pieces of blubber and other whale parts would then be cut out using flensing knives - razor sharp blades maybe one to two feet long on the ends of ten-foot handles – then hauled aboard using block and tackles to allow further cutting up and processing. Our new *Australis* also had winches which would do this more easily than by teams of men.

The great advantage to this method was that the whale could easily be rolled over by use of the ropes and winches. The disadvantages included the precarious position of the flensers at the beginning of the process who would have to lean out over the side of the platform or even step onto the carcass to carve it up. The other difficulties included that of wielding such long knives in a small space and hoping that most of the whale or the vessel or both would remain stable. Flensing was all but impossible if the sea started to get rough at all. There was also the added excitement that the flensing might attract sharks that would launch themselves at the whale carcass and bite of great chunks of meat or blubber while the flensers went about their work. All of this was joy to Captain Tobey, as he saw the advantages in having a larger platform on which to cut up and process the whale. Andersen also pointed out that there were a row of very efficient try-pots – large covered kettles sitting on formed brick bases just before the mainmast in a row which extended across the deck. The exhaust from the fires in these brick fireplaces would be channelled by flues into the single, tall smokestack which stood behind the mainmast midway between it and the mizzenmast. Below the boom of the spanker[6] was a low deckhouse with portholes along each of its sides. This ran from behind the mainmast to almost the stern of the vessel with the funnel, mizzenmast and two small skylights in the roof. At the stern, it ended in a small wheelhouse, raised slightly above the level of the deckhouse just aft of the end of the boom. Peder Andersen was very proud of this innovation, for it was still the convention that a vessel's wheel should be both at the stern and open to the elements. Many captains, and indeed my father, was one of them, believed that the helmsmen should have a wide view of the vessel, its sails and the sea. This had been the tradition since sailing vessels first went to sea. In Peder Andersen's practical mind, having served many years in the Arctic whaling trade, there was no purpose in the lone helmsman suffering the wind and spray at temperatures below zero. After all, he reasoned, it was the helmsman's task to watch the lubber line[7] of the compass and keep the vessel on course. The officer-of-the-watch and the rest of the watch had the responsibility of looking where they were going and what might be in the way of its passage. This new wheelhouse had been accepted as a compromise by my father who had eventually come

---

[6] This is the large, quadrilateral sail carried in line with the vessel's axis, which is fore-and-aft. It is gaff-rigged, that is, it has a spar at top to hold the sail which is raised up the mizzenmast at the stern of the ship. An additional triangular topsail may be hoisted above this.

[7] A lubber line is a fixed line on a compass binnacle pointing towards the front of the ship or and corresponding to the craft's centreline (being the customary direction of movement).

around to Andersen's suggestion. I am sure that father's bad experiences in his last cruise in the *Aquinnah* played some part in his change of heart.

When we came on board, Andersen was keen to show us the innovations in this new vessel. The wheelhouse had windows along its front which could be dropped down giving an open view to the rest of the vessel. This no doubt pleased father, but the back of the wheelhouse was flush with the stern timbers and was entered from the deck by two entrances which were also open but could be covered by rolls of canvas which came down from its overhanging roof. Within the deckhouse there was a large ship's wheel aft of a large binnacle[8] and several small dials to show the engine's steam pressure and rate of revolutions of the propeller. There was also a trumpet-like brass speaking tube which would enable the officer-of-the-watch or the captain to speak directly to the engineer. Andersen also pointed out a row of small pipes below the wheel.

"These are heating tubes," he said. "They are fed with steam from the boilers and can be used to keep the helmsman warm at night." He laughed at this extravagance. "Better for him when you are in the ice, Ja?"

On either side of the binnacle there were two hatches leading down below into the deckhouse. Looking down the

---

[8] The columnar structure which holds the compass and is often internally illuminated by a small lamp to show the compass' surface.

one at the left or portside, I could see a small hutch containing a chart rack and small table – the chartroom. At its end was a door which Andersen said lead into the officers' quarters. We descended the small ladder of the hatch to the right or starboard side of the binnacle and found ourselves to be in another cabin. This contained a large desk with a comfortable chair bolted to the floor and several racks which already contained some charts, a brass telescope and several nautical almanacs. This, Andersen called the 'Captains Day Cabin' which was, in fact the working office of the captain and doubled as a chartroom. We went through this cabin through another internal door and into the main captain's cabin. This was spacious compared to others which I had visited when father commanded my previous vessels and contained a small stove in one corner, a table and bench built into to one bulkhead[9] and a good-sized bunk on the other side. Two portholes in each side and a glass skylight above gave ample illumination although there were several lamps gimballed above the table and bunk.

Continuing through this cabin and up through a small hatch, we came out upon the main deck just before the mainmast. Here Miss Andersen was waiting for us. Father and Mr. Andersen continued to walk forward along the deck engrossed in animated conversation. My hand was suddenly grasped and I looked into the lovely hazel eyes of Liv Andersen.

---

[9] Bulkheads are the walls of cabins in ships.

"Come!" she said. "I will show you around your new ship."
I was slightly taken aback by this forthright and outgoing
young girl. Her attentions were at odds with the behaviour
of those few girls whom I had met in my native Nantucket
where formal Yankee customs had been made even more
closed by the influence of the town's Quaker foundation.

I did not find her manner unpleasant so I allowed her to
hold my hand and lead me across the deck.

"See!" she said, pointing to the row of try-pots just forward
of the mainmast. "You have four beautiful pots, here. Each
one holds six hundred litres and below their furnaces is a
trough of water to keep you from burning your deck. Father
has also rigged them with steam pipes direct from the boiler
if you wish to use that heat, too. And the outlets can be
fitted with the hose also"

I was very impressed by the girl's knowledge and pride in
her father's work. "And look here!" she continued. "You
have steam-powered winches to haul the whale on deck or
the spars aloft. You can use the power of the steam or you
can do it the hard way by hand."

We walked past the broad central deck which now
contained six whale boats stacked behind the foremast in
two tiers of three along the deck adjacent to their two sets
of removable davits[10] which could be removed when the
deck was being cleared for whale processing. I had also

---

[10] These are light weight crane-like devices used on a ship for supporting, raising, and
lowering boats over the side. On the *Australis* these are removable with their ends fitted
into supports flush with the deck just inside of the bulwarks.

noticed earlier in our tour that there was a small Jolly Boat hung from fixed davits across the stern of the vessel behind the wheelhouse.

Just forward of the foremast, was the foc'sle. This was where the bow of the vessel had been raised to form a large, triangular cabin which could be entered by two hatches on either side of the deck. This was to be the home of most of our crew – the captain and his officers being housed in their quarters below the deckhouse at the stern. It was often said by some crews about their relationship with the officer class that 'aft the most honour but forward the better man'.

We knocked on the starboard hatch and entered for we knew that some of our crew were now working as that this was their domain. Lars our happy Norwegian carpenter was sitting at the table nearby and turned, his face broadening in smile.

"Åh, velkommen![11]" he said, swinging his arm across his body to indicate that we should enter.

"Takk så mye![12]" replied Liv Andersen with a laugh, for she easily switched from English to her native Norwegian which they call Norsk.

The large triangular cabin had been fitted with several partitions inside of which our crew could store their seaman's chests and swing their hammocks when sleeping. They were empty now and the rolled hammocks were

---

[11] "Oh welcome" (to several persons) in Norse.
[12] "Thanks so much!" in Norse

stored in long bins below each of the two central tables which ran down the centre of the cabin. In the centre of the sizeable space between the tables was a small pot-bellied stove which would provide some comfort and some personal cooking facilities for the men.

A hatch in the deck led down to the storerooms below. There was plenty of space here for our large supply of food and barrels of fresh water. A short companionway out of the storerooms led to a spacious galley where Jacob Simmons our cook was inspecting the new stove. It was a marvellous affair of cast iron and was much larger than those of previous ships on which I had served - and served was the right word for it! As cabin boy to my father, I often had to go down to the galley to fetch the hot food on a cold winter's night, but that was welcome just to keep warm for a short time whilst the cook dished out the 'salt junk'[13] or whatever was on the menu for that night. This galley stove consisted of a generous oven with built-in boiler on the other side of a large firebox which was fuel with wood. The top of the stove consisted of a wide hotplate edged with a high railing to prevent any pots from sliding off during any sort of a sea. At one end of the hotplate was a large tank in which water was heated with a brass tap hanging over the edge. Mr Simmons was very happy with his galley for there was considerable space in the form of racks, enclosed shelves and cupboards into which he could store the more

---

[13] Salt Junk was the sailor's term for salted meat (pork or beef) or fish which was preserved in salt and kept in barrels for storage. It was commonly boiled in the galley's stove in bulk.

delicate items of his trade. Large pans, kettles and pots were hung on large hooks near the stove.

We moved on further aft into the main storage area of the vessel. This consisted of several large holds which were now empty save for the bulk store hold which held casks of fresh water, salted meat, dry food stuffs and the carpenter's and bo's'n's[14] stores which had already been partly supplied with all of the spare spars, timbers, ropes, blocks and other paraphernalia which were needed around a vessel of this size. Next came the huge hold which was now empty but would hold the hogsheads[15] which could be filled with oil and other liquids boiled down from the seals and whales we hoped to catch. There was also another hold aft of this which would be used for storing seal skins and whalebone.

Finally, walking further aft we came to the smaller coal bunkers, separated partitions on each side of the vessel from whence came the coal for our steam boiler nearby. Beyond this and the root of the mainmast was our engine room. The engine room was larger than I had imagined, taking up most of the depth of the hull. To me this was a marvellous new world. A world of mechanical things, pipes, pistons and cylinder heads painted in green with round glass gauges looking like big eyes peering into the darkness beyond the passageways on each side of the three

---

[14] The bo's'n or boatswain was the officer on-board responsible for all of the boats and general deck rigging of the ship.
[15] Large cylindrical wooden containers (barrels were the smaller size) which usually held about 54 imperial gallons or 64 American gallons (about 245 litres).

massive cylinders of our compound engine. This was Hamish Dunsmuir's world - a world of heat, noise and the smell of coal - a world that engineers love and guard with great jealousy from those lesser creatures of the upper deck. The worthy engineer himself was busily adjusting a small screw on one of the pressure gauges so did not hear our approach even in the unusual silence of his new domain.

"You can see that Erik Sørensen has calibrated your boiler to a safe limit of two hundred eighty pounds per square inch." Said a quiet female voice from behind us. Engineer Dunsmuir spun around quickly; his eyes wide from being not only interrupted from his concentration but by the uncommon sound of a female voice in an engine room – his engine room.

His angry face softened when he looked into the smiling face of Liv Andersen. "Och! ye did friten me, lassie. Aye, it wull dae us braw. Bit ta!"[16]

I smiled to myself when I first met Hamish Dunsmuir before sailing across with father and the small crew. Our meeting was very formal. As I shook his hand in welcome he had replied in his thick accent "Please tae mak' yer aquaintence, young sur." This was difficult to catch even though the words were common enough and I had then replied with some delight, "My pleasure, Mr Dunsmuir, and from what part of Scotland do you hail?" The look on

---

[16] "Oh, you did frighten me young lady. Yes, it will do fine. But thank you."

his face had changed to something akin to distaste and he replied with some earnestness "I dae nae come fae Scootlund. A'm a Canadian!" which put me very much in my place for Hamish Dunsmuir was from Nova Scotia where they still spoke a purer form of the Scottish language than any jock north of the border.

We left Mr Dunsmuir to his confusion at meeting a pretty young girl who also knew something about engines to go up on deck. There was a gentle but crisp north-western breeze blowing down the fjord as father and I escorted the Andersen's to one of their boats waiting near the stern exit way.

"A good afternoon, Captain Tobey! I wish you a pleasant first night aboard your new vessel," said Peder Andersen. "We will see you soon as you and your men will have a lot to do."

Father nodded and waved his hand as he saw them over the side. All I could do was raise a hand to the pretty girl now sitting in the stern sheets[17] of the boat.

---

[17] The aft or end part of a small open boat

Chapter Five
Homeward Bound

Latitude 57° 58' 48" North; Longitude 23° 52' 12" West
52⁰F, winds 35 knots, fresh gale from the West

Our stay in Bergen had suddenly become too short. The last week was a maelstrom of activity with the final preparations for our departure. I saw Liv Andersen only at painfully short moments for she, too had urgent duties within the shipyard.

The last night ashore followed a day of farewells to all of our friends that we had made in the lovely city of Bergen. Erik and Jørn Halvorsen at the hotel wished us well and provided us with an excellent hamper of food and the men at Andersen's shipyard had all gathered to say farewell. I saw Liv Andersen at the dinner which her father and some of the dignitaries had organised in the reception room of the Rådhus or Town Hall. There were many speeches, starting with the Borgermester[18] of Bergen and ending in father's long-winded speech of thanks and farewell. Liv Andersen had been seated with her father on the other side of the Borgermester who held the seat of honour in the centre of the head table, so it was not until the end of dinner, when the men retired to the smoking room and the ladies to the lounge that I had a few fleeting moments with

---

[18] The Mayor

her on the terrace where we held hands and promised that we would meet again one day.

In the morning, Jørn Halvorsen brought our things from his father's hotel from where we had a boatman take them out to the *Australis*. Our small crew had already taken their meagre possessions from the Seaman's Mission and were already aboard. Mr Dunsmuir had fired up the vessel's boiler and advised us when we went on board that the engine was ready. The single propeller had been lowered from its protective well, the sails had all been furled and our two anchors had been raised.

With everything ready on board, father waved to the large crowd of workers and their families who had gathered on and around the slipway to Andersen's yard. That worthy gentleman and his lovely daughter stood at the edge of the slipway and waved back. I raised my arm in a forlorn attempt to say farewell but I had wished to some degree that our stay was much longer.

Father walked into the small wheelhouse, gave the helmsman a wink and blew down the brass voice pipe which connected the wheelhouse to the engine room. "You may start your engine, Mr. Dunsmuir. Slow ahead, if you please." He turned to our helmsman Tobias Henry "Steady as you go, Tobias. Steer two-seventy, we don't want to hit yonder point."

As the *Australis* slowly made its way from its birth-anchorage, father reached up and pulled at a small brass-capped cord which hung from the roof of the wheelhouse. There was a loud, high pitched note sounding in the air and a small jet of steam issued from the whistle which was near the top of our slim funnel which now belched a huge amount of black smoke. A steam whistle! What an excitement for all of those aboard and on shore who were used to the quiet departure of sailing vessels.

Slowly the *Australis* came around and headed west passed the Vågen, the narrow bay around which the city of Bergen was developing and out into the wide Byfjorden , the fjord which separates the island of Askøy from the mainland. Soon we turned south to negotiate the narrows between the islands of Sotra and Bjorøyna then into the main shipping channel which led to the open sea.

Free at last! Into the open sea and winds with little between us and our home shores but the North Atlantic. Father had considered taking the traditional trade wind route home by sailing well to the south, past Britain and then turning west after stopping at the Canary Islands. By doing this we would avoid sailing into the prevailing westerlies of the northern route directly across the North Atlantic. Taking this northern route would also mean sailing against the Gulf Stream current which runs northward along the coast of America and then crosses the Atlantic into European waters. Whilst the traditional southern route would probably offer more easy sailing, the passage would take a significantly longer period of time. Instead father decided to take the shorter, more difficult route directly across the North Atlantic on a south-westerly course against both the westerly winds and the Gulf Stream. He reasoned that the *Australis* was a stout and handy vessel and even with a reduced crew could easily tack[19] across the wind. Moreover, if the winds and current were too adverse then we would strike all sail and use our engine to navigate the most direct route home. Whilst this would be harder, and the northern route was more prone to storms, it would be the quickest route. As winter was fast approaching, father wanted to cross the Atlantic as soon as possible.

Anyone living on board a vessel soon becomes attuned to its every motion and sounds of the sea and the wind. The sounds of water against the hull can vary from a gentle hiss to a jarring repetitive bump; the wind rushing through the standing rigging can be a low, comforting gentle murmur or load shrieks that would terrify all who heard it. Then of course, the motions of sea and wind will cause the vessel to have its own way of behaving, from a docile creature running steadily before a gentle breeze to a raging, writhing and tortured beast with a heaving deck and a masthead gyrating in a rapid figure-of-eight pattern.

---

[19] Tack – a sailing vessel, whose desired course is into the wind, turns its bow alternatively across the wind's direction so that the wind will strike the sails from a side angle allowing progress in the desired direction.

Something was not right! It was still dark but the morning watch had come on deck as I had not slept well and had been awake at eight bells.

The vessel was heaving more violently than before and the sea thumped loudly under the hull. The tilt of the cabin told me that we were hull over and on the port tack. Quickly I put on my oilskins and sea boots and went out on deck. The *Australis* was heeled well over with the wind blowing from the west onto our port side at gale force. The sails had been shortened so that we carried only our topsails with a single reefed and the topgallant sails and royals had been furled. All of the staysails had been taken in save for the jibs. I suddenly heard my father close at hand. "Get that flying jib down smartly now!" He was standing above me on the roof of the deckhouse and holding on to the pinrail of the mizzenmast. Seeing me come on deck he gestured forward and yelled against the wind. "Jamie, go for'ard and help those men on the jibs!"

"Aye, sir!" I replied and made my way forward along the wet and heaving deck. I grasped the first jacklines[20] which had been rigged fore-and-aft along the deck between the mizzen and Main and slowly hauled myself forward. The wind was incredibly strong and occasionally a wave of green water would break over the side to sweep me off my feet. Clambering up to the starboard ladder of the raised

---

[20] Jacklines are safety lines or ropes secured strongly at points along the decks so that sailors could keep a good hold.

foc'sle, I made my way along to where a small group of men was endeavouring to take down the flying jib, the foremost of the large triangular sails at the bow. To do this, the sheet which was used to haul up the sail had been let go and the men were now hauling the large sail down the forestay which ran from the end of the bowsprit to near the top of the foremast. The sail was held onto this stay by small hooks called hanks. Three of the men were low to the deck pulling in the jib and folding it onto the deck. The fourth, the big Pole Krystof, was having some difficulties undoing the hanks on the stiff canvas.

"Avast! Hold on for ya' lives"! Came a sudden cry from one of the men. Instantly I grasped the rail which ran along the bowsprit and acted as a jackstay as the bow of the *Australis* suddenly dipped at an alarmingly steep angle into an on-coming wall of green water. The three crew at my side saw the large swell rising up and ran back along the deck of the foc'sle and jumped down onto the main deck. I saw the end of the bowsprit, with Krystof still grimly holding onto the forestay, dig into the wall of water which came rushing along the spar and crashed onto the raised foc'sle deck where I was standing. Knocked to the deck as water surged past, I managed to grasp the port jackline and held on for my life. It seemed an eternity in time as the bow of our vessel dug deeply into the oncoming crest and for a time I thought that we would continue being driven down into the depths. Then suddenly, as though the *Australis* objected to this drenching, she lifted her bow and rose boldly up again. Lying stretched out on the small deck and holding the jackline in both hands I looked up and saw Krystof rising bodily out of the green water like some fugitive from Neptune's realm. The brave Pole still clung to the forestay, his arms and legs wrapped around it with the pile of tangled canvas below. His long hair ran with water and he looked at me with shock and horror in his eyes. But he had survived being submerged at least fifteen feet below the water.

His three watch mates had clambered back up onto the deck. "See to him before he is washed off!" I yelled and they hauled the big man back onto the deck where all hung on to each other and laughed at the predicament of the hapless seaman. With one eye on the rollers which were battering into the bow of our little vessel, the men quickly overcame their fear and successfully hauled down the flying jib before dragging the canvas down to the lower deck where it could be folded more safely.

I made my way back to the aft deckhouse where father still stood like the ancient mariner he was. "I see you had an Atlantic shower?" he said with a grin on his weather-beaten face. "Go to the wheelhouse and see to our course". It was six bells in the morning watch and there was a grey glimmer of light in the east.

The North Atlantic can be a fickle ocean prone to be stormy and dangerous at the best of times. With the warm waters of the Gulf Stream ocean current flowing northward from the Caribbean and the cold wind temperatures of the north, storms are the most likely outcome. At times, however it can be incredibly beautiful and benign. Only a few days after our vessel had been crashing through the deep troughs of oncoming rollers and battling to tack into the face of a howling gale, the wind abated and the sky cleared. The wind was now very gentle and the sea was like a flexible sheet of translucent green glass. There were still the faint remains of the turbulence of the previous days but now the waves were more like a series of large, rounded green hills which heaved this way and that, reflecting the sunlight from each changing surface. The *Australis* easily rose up and then down over these rounded hills; sometimes up on a large crest so that our stern came clear of the water, and next rolling down into a smooth valley of a trough with green sides all around. It was a glorious day with most of the hands busying themselves around the deck securing parts which had come adrift, coiling the many lines which had been rigged for safety and repairing the slight damage which had occurred during the storm. Father took a sighting with our sextant at noon despite the heaving of the deck and found that we were closer to the American mainland than we had hoped. With the wind now backing further to the northeast he estimated that we should round Cape Spear within ten more days of good sailing.

Father's navigation had always been excellent and so it was on the eleventh day, we rounded that most easterly cape of Newfoundland and sailed a direct course southwest to Nantucket Island. Rounding that faithful old signpost to home, we sailed westward past Martha's Vineyard and then tacked northeast into Buzzard Bay which lay in front of our beloved New Bedford. On passing Mishaum Point, which is only five nautical miles from home, father ordered that all sails be dropped and that our engine be started. Mister Dunsmuir was delighted with this order and promptly had his stokers raise the steam pressure in the boiler accordingly. Father intended to show off our new and modern *Australis* by taking her into the New Bedford harbour under steam power alone. With Fort Phoenix on our starboard beam, father gave our steam whistle several long blasts. "This will shake them up!" he said with some pride. Sure enough! As soon as we came into sight of the main harbour, a huge crowd had gathered on the docks and promontories of the city. The word had quickly spread that Captain Tobey had returned from the sea.

Chapter Six
Course 180⁰ - South

Latitude 00°; Longitude 16° 20' 10" West
89⁰F, winds very slight 1-3 knots from the East but variable

Our homecoming was a joyous affair; for the people of New Bedford it heralded a new beginning for the whaling trade and prosperity; for our crew it meant a short rest from the sea; and for my mother it meant the relief that father would honour his agreement with her and at last retire from the sea. For myself I was happy to be home again and was both elated and apprehensive that I was to be given command of this beautiful new vessel and carry on the Tobey tradition.

The Mayor had organised a civic banquet in the town hall at which my family and I were the guests of honour. Many of the town's dignitaries were also there and many speeches were made – mostly by the Mayor. The last to speak was my father. He thanked the Mayor and the good people of New Bedford for their fine reception and predicted that there would be a new prosperity once whaling ships such as the *Australis* put to sea. There were audible gasps as father outlined his plan for whaling in Antarctic waters which would mean longer periods of time that whalers would be from their families with the new hardships which the crews would have to endure. He also proposed that an Antarctic Whaling Company be established and plans be drawn up for several more vessels like the *Australis* and even permanent whaling 'stations' (as he called them) be set up to provide better processing of the whales and for better comfort of the men on a safe shore. Whilst there seemed to be much enthusiasm for the building of new auxiliary steamers for the whaling trade, there was less enthusiasm for going to Antarctica. The good people of New Bedford were well used to the hardships of their men going to sea in pursuit of the great whale but were conservative as to how this should be done. At the end of father's speech, he bade me to stand and proudly acknowledged me as the new captain of the *Australis*. There were many 'hurrahs' and applause, but somehow I felt that it was almost too much. Besides, the festivities had reminded me of my last farewell from the lovely girl of Bergen.

The next few weeks became a frantic race to equip the *Australis* with all the necessities needed for her long voyage south. Father had hand-picked a good crew who were eager for such an adventurous undertaking. As the whaling trade had suffered a significant downturn there were experienced whalers aplenty around New Bedford. Of course, he chose the most experienced men including Caleb Warren, his old friend and former first mate of father's ill-fated *Aquinnah*. He would again be in that position as my second-in-command with Joseph Turling who had come across from the *Norfolk Lass* as our second mate. Of course, Hamish Dunsmuir was our engineer and he brought with him John Stevens as his second engineer. The rest of the crew were seasoned whalers including our six harpooners. These were a mixed bag of very independent types who had hunted the whale for many years. Five were native

New Englanders including Joseph Miantumi who was of the Narragansett tribe from Rhode Island whose ancestors had hunted the whale before the Europeans arrived. The sixth harpooner was a large and friendly Pacific Islander called Taumalolo who always had a broad smile on his face, especially when things were not going well. The rest of the crew – there were fifty-five officers and men all told – included some of father's old crew including the solid Norwegian, Lars the carpenter, Tobias Henry our dour quartermaster, Jacob Simmons the cook and the Pole, Krystof, our most sturdy hand.

Now we had six strong whaleboats stacked in two groups of three, lashed astern of the foremast. These were light thirty feet long and six feet wide. They had been built for speed and manoeuvrability being double ended and of shallow depth. They were of a simple design making them strong and easy to repair. In Bergen, Peder Andersen had laughed and suggested that he had made us six small longships in the Viking style as they had been constructed out of oak, Thor's most favoured timber. However, he had constructed the hulls with planks which were nailed and caulked flush to each other and not overlapped as in clinker-built hulls of the old style. Like the old longships, our whalers were also equipped with a mast, sail, were powered by five sixteen- to eighteen-foot long oars and steered with a twenty-two-foot-long steering oar.

On board the *Australis*, we kept the traditional three-watch system[21]. Each watch consisted of two whaleboat crews made up of six men. The boat crews were commanded by a "boatheader" – in the *Australis* these were Caleb Warren, Joseph Turling and two of our most senior hands. The whaleboat crew also included a harpooner and four foremast hands. The harpooner pulled the forward oar in approaching a whale. After harpooning and getting fast to it, he went aft and steered the boat as the whale sped off. When the poor creature finally tired, the commander of the whaleboat would then move forward to wield the lance and kill the whale.

Having taken on a vast quantity of salted, dried and otherwise preserved food, freshwater and other provisions for our survival, we also loaded a spare set of sails, bulk canvas, spars and other timbers which would be needed in order to replace any parts of our vessel which may be damaged during our voyage. Our vessel also carried two sextants and chronometers, a spare boat compass and the most accurate sets of navigation almanacs. In addition, father had equipped us with a comprehensive library of known charts, astronomical tables and books about

---

[21] The watch-keeping crew, as opposed to the idlers who do not keep watch such as the carpenter, cook and others who worked throughout the day and had the night off, could be divided into three watches giving each sailor more time off-duty. Naming schemes such as foremast, mainmast and mizzen are common. Each watch stood a four-hour shift starting at First Watch at 8 pm except for the Dog Watches which were two hours each started at four pm. The Dog Watches allowed an uneven number of watches so that sailors would not be rostered onto the same one each day. The term may have come from the fact that in the early evening at about these times, Sirius, the Dog Star in the constellation of Canis Major (the Great Dog) is the first one to be seen.

Antarctic waters as he could find. Works of great navigators and explorers such as James Cook, Fabian von Bellingshausen, James Clark Ross and James Weddell had been collected as well as copies of many of the journals of sealers such as Palmer, Powell and Davis who had also ventured across the Antarctic Circle.

The weather in New Bedford was beginning to change as we were now at the start of fall with a cold north wind and drizzle blowing in from Canada. All things being satisfactorily stowed, we slowly departed Merrill's Wharf early on the morning of the 23rd day of October, 1845. Despite the wind and rain, there was a goodly crowd of the citizenry of New Bedford as well as the families of the crew on the wharf to see us away. My mother and father stood where our gangway had been, mother trying hard not to weep and father, grim-faced trying to shelter her under his oilskins.
"Have a safe voyage, Jamie" he had said quietly. "There's no rescue in the Antarctic."

My last vision of my parents was of the huddled pair and father raising his arm in farewell. It was difficult not to shed a tear, as many of my men lined the side and waved and yelled their 'good byes' to their own loved ones. I held back my tears as I stood on top of the aft deckhouse.

"Watch your helm, Mr Henry! Hands to clear harbour!" I called in turning towards the stern.

This had been quite unnecessary as Tobias Henry knew this wharf and harbour better than most, but I needed to tear myself away from a sad farewell and the men at the side needed an excuse to leave their sadness behind ashore.

Thus, we steamed out of New Bedford's safe harbour and into the expanse of Buzzards Bay. The sound of our steam whistle and our thin plume of black smoke drifted across the water as a last gesture of farewell.

"Steer southwest if you please, Mr. Henry!" I said, jumping down off the roof of the deckhouse and entering the small shelter which was the wheelhouse. "We'll pick up our coal at Norfolk, Virginia in three days, then you can show me how to steer".

"Aye, Cap'n, that I will" he said with a wide grin, for it was known that he could only be happy at his wheel in the expanses of the open sea.

We made good time steaming into the Hampton roads and docking at Lambert's Point ready to take on coal on the morning of the third day. Here was a rail line which brought good steaming coal from the mines of the Appalachians right into Norfolk. There was no rest, however, for the men to visit this bustling little city for there was coal to be loaded. Every man who could be spared was now busy shovelling the sooty black coal into burlap sacks at the open coal wagons on the wharf or carrying the heavy bags on board and into our coal bunkers below. Here, Mr.

Dunsmuir the engineer supervised the stacking of the bags with the precise eye and occasional caustic remark that only an engineer could who was proud and over-protective of his shiny new engine.

"Dinnae drap it thare, ye oaf. Stack it neatly!" became the cry of the day for the men held Mr. Dunsmuir in great esteem, despite his scouring and hard words. Eventually, by the end of the day, the bunkers of the *Australis* were full of coal and there also were many piles of coal bags stacked neatly upon the main deck.

Taking advantage of a westerly evening land breeze, we sailed out of the Hampton Roads and out into the open sea, passing the Fisherman's Island light at the start of the First Watch[22]. Our course was southeast as we had planned to sail directly across the North Atlantic to the Cape Verde Islands with a short stop in Bermuda. The hurricane season would almost be over and we would have the consistent North East Trade Winds on our port tack for most of the way. In addition, if we sailed a little to the north of our destination, we might be able to pick up the Canary Current coming south. From the Cape Verde Islands, our intended course would then be East Sou'east so that we would make landfall off the north-eastern coast of Brazil and then sail down the coast to the port of São Salvador da Bahia. This port was well suited for our purposes for it was a well-developed whaling port where we would be able restock

---

[22] At 8 pm.

our vessel. Moreover, it lies on a bay, which I am told by the older whalers of New Bedford, which is a well-known breeding ground of whales.

Our passage to the Cape Verde Islands was generally uneventful and the crew became well-satisfied with our long tack across this part of the Atlantic which gave us its best behaviour. The North Atlantic was well-known for its troublesome storms but our voyage was blessed with the good, strong and consistent Trades which took the *Australis* steadily east and south until we reached the port of Mindelo on the island of São Vicente which was a coaling port for British shipping.

Our stay here was short being of only two days duration. Here we were able to give the crew a short period of leave on shore and also to take on some more supplies including a little additional coal due to the generosity of the British coaling station. Having cleared all of the formalities with the local Portuguese authorities, we set sail and headed South sou'west.

We had been in tropical waters for some time but now we headed into the area known as the 'doldrums'. Here the Northeast Trade Winds met the Southeast Trades giving a vast area a little north of the Equator where winds were slight and at times non-existent. On some days we hoisted all of our sails including our large staysails between our fore- and main masts. When the wind dropped completely, I gave orders that our engine be started as a result we did not suffer the traditional frustrations which plagued earlier sailors who depended upon sail alone, often spending days drifting aimlessly over a flat sea; the only way to move would be to lower the boats and tow their vessel by the power of muscle and oar.

Whilst Mr. Dunsmuir grumbled that we were using up his precious supplies of coal, we all knew that he was proud that his engine would carry our lovely vessel across a sea where the sails would hang limp and windless for days. It was a slow passage but a happy one. The men delighted in the quiet days with smooth seas and only the gentle breeze due to our own mobility blowing along our deck. Days were pleasant, devoted to making and mending both the vessels needs and those of the crew. All sails had been taken down and for some of the older hands there was a sense of concerned wonder about a vessel at sea moving across the ocean without any sail being set. Most of the crew were occupied with the many small tasks which went on aboard when times were more relaxed. New ratlines were fitted to replace those which had frayed or broken; there were ropes to be spliced; blocks to be checked and of course the exposed timbers of railings and boats were given an additional coating of preservative. Out on our main deck space, between the two forward masts, our sailmaker, Ezekiel Chapman, was busily repairing a small tear in the clew of our large Nock Staysail[23].

---

[23] This is the lower, rear corner of the large triangular sail raised high between the two forward masts.

There were days when the sea was like rolling hills of green glass – sparkling as the sunlight danced upon the water. The air was warm and the sky was a light blue. Often a pod of dolphins would come up to our bow and ride the waves created by our motion. They are glorious animals with their sleek, grey bodies glistening in the sun, diving and surfacing just in front of our bow waves. At times I forgot that I was captain of the vessel and left my responsibilities with the Officer-of-the-Watch and, climbing down into the netting below the bowsprit, I lay there and watched the antics of these masters of the sea.

When the sun set and if there was no moon, the stars above sparkled like small twinkling lights with an intensity and clarity not usually seen in the mist covered parts of our native New England waters. There were stars of different brightness, in colours of white, blues, orange and red which were all reflected in the smooth shiny, undulating sea. Standing aft on the roof of the deckhouse, I would hold onto a stay and look up at this majestic canopy and the blackness of our masts and rigging swinging lazily in small circles. Only our single white masthead light gleamed brighter than the stars above.

So, we slowly progressed south. Sometimes there would be a cry from the masthead 'Wind ho! Off the starboard beam!' and a light zephyr would shake out the wrinkles in our limp sails; but no more than that. At other times we would use our engine after furling all of our sails only to hear the masthead cry which took all hands to the yards. Eventually we crossed the Equator at the thirty-degree west meridian.

It was here that we held the traditional ceremony of Crossing the Line. It was suggested to me one evening by Joseph Turling, our second mate who had served with the British navy before 'securing better quarters' (his words) in an American whaler many year ago. After a brief discussion with Mr Warren, we decided that it would be good for morale as many of the Yankees of our crew had never been this far south and our lack of wind action in the doldrums had cursed us all with a fit of boredom. And so it was that one night a casual 'conversation' amongst the crew delivered up a list of potential 'Pollywogs' – for this is the traditional name for those 'scurvy dogs and landlubbers' who had never crossed the equator before. For a brief moment, I feared that my inexperience at sea would mean that my name would be added to the list, such was the good sense of camaraderie and democracy of the crew of the *Australis*, but my first mate, Caleb Warren, being a wise man as well as a good sailor suggested that the Captain was required to be present at such a ceremony in full dress uniform in order to welcome 'King Nepture' aboard as his personal guest. For this, I breathed a quiet sigh of relief.

Accordingly, early the next morning at the ringing of the eighth bell at the end of the morning watch[24] there was a

------

[24] 8 am.

series of good-natured scuffles around the vessel as men who had been deemed Trusty Shellbacks because they had already crossed the line in other vessels, pounced upon their hapless mess-mates. These Pollywogs then had their hands tied behind their backs, blindfolded and led to the main deck.

They were huddled in a small and writhing group by the foremast where they were told that they must await our august visitor. Mr Turling produced his old Navy Bosun's Call[25] and gave a long, high note to gain the attention of all hands that our guest, good King Neptune was coming aboard. Suddenly, up through the port gangway came a most bizarre figure. This was King Neptune who had come aboard to welcome all of the new initiates to his watery world. The figure was dressed in a ragged toga of coarse blue calico and was smeared all over with a blue dye of some sort. Upon his head he wore a shiny metal crown of beaten and cut copper and he held a long flensing tool, this being considered more appropriate to a whaling ship than a mere trident, the traditional staff of Neptune. Despite the outlandish garb, King Neptune bore a remarkable resemblance to Kristof our good-natured Pole.

---

[25] A brass whistle used to give signals at sea. Here he would pipe the 'Still an eight-second-long blast to bring all hands to attention. Especially when a visitor comes aboard. Once the welcome has been made, the 'carry-on' is piped as a short high note dropping suddenly to a longer low note would be made. Normally this would not be done on a whaling ship.

Following closely behind came his royal Queen, Amphitrite, one of our young apprentices dressed also in a long blue makeshift dress and a high crown of silver made from card placed over curls of wood shavings painted yellow to look like hair. Over the side there next appeared the fearsome assistant of his watery highness in the form of Davy Jones. He was indeed a fearsome sight. A huge man with naturally dark skin and his body heavily tattooed all over. He too wore an elaborate headpiece of rope ends painted silver and carried a long harpoon. His face was set in a permanent scowl except when he ejected his black tongue out and over his chin. This awesome figure was in fact our chief harpooner, Taumalolo our giant harpooner from the Pacific isles.

After our distinguished guest had been seated upon his throne (an armchair from the officer's saloon covered in a rich mat) and his retinue gathered around, the Pollywogs were addressed by the giant attendant, Davy Jones. Taumalolo did this in his lilting English with words of his native tongue as a high song denigrating their crimes against the watery kingdom. The Pollywogs were accused of all sorts of heinous crimes: of being still attached to the land as landlubbers; of failing to learn all of the skills of good sailormen; of failing to honour the great fishes of the sea; and above all, of showing disrespect to the King of the Water himself by keeping to themselves in the cold waters of the northern ice.

"E hoʻolohe mai iaʻu, e nā hoaaloha a pau o ke kai.[26]." Sang Taumalolo. "What is it that we should do for these?"

"Kiss the fish an' wet'em all over!" called the Shellbacks. "Let's 'ave 'em!"

Now, in turn, each Pollywog was made to submit himself to the royal party on his knees. Davy Jones would step forward with a large fish which had been caught that morning and the unfortunate victim would have to kiss the dead creature. After this, he would be grabbed by several of the Shellbacks and dragged over to one of the try pots which would normally be used to boil down the whale blubber. Here he would have his hair and face liberally smeared with a mixture of fish oil and lard from the Galley stove before his upper body was upended in the pot. Left a while to flounder upon the deck, the victim had his hands released and his blindfold removed.
"Hurrah!" cried his messmates who would run to lift their newly initiated comrade upon their shoulders and convey him to the aft deckhouse roof where he could sit in state and watch the rest of the Pollywogs get their treatment.

With all of the Pollywogs now converted to Shellbacks, the crew enjoyed a festive day as the weather was warm and mild and the sea calm. After a little personal make and mend, the crew set up a small canvas stage in the centre of the main deck, lanterns were tied up in the rigging and a general festive air prevailed. Two of the men produced

---

[26] "Oh hear me all of the friends of the sea"

fiddles and one a tin whistle and together our small band played a series of well-known sea shanties to the assembled crew, many of whom jumped up upon the stage and performed various hornpipes[27].

The song which all applauded was the popular Yankee Whaler which was a Halyard Shanty to be sung as the watches hauled on the halyards or ropes which raised, lowered or turned the yards which held the sails:

A Yankee ship came down the river,
Blow, boys, blow,
A Yankee ship came down the river,
Blow, boys, bully boys, blow.

And how do you know she's a Yankee whaler?
Blow, boys, blow,
Oh, how do you know she's a Yankee whaler?
Blow, boys, bully boys, blow.

The stars and bars they flew behind her,
Blow, boys, blow.
The stars and bars they flew behind her.
Blow, boys, bully boys, blow.

And who do you think was the skipper of her?
Blow, boys, blow.

---

[27] Lively sailor's dance often done by one man or sometimes by groups in unison often with arms folded.

A bluenosed son of a hardcase whaler;
Blow, boys, bully boys, blow.

And who do you think was the chief mate of her?
Blow, boys, blow.
An old loud salt of a New Bedford sailor.
Blow, boys, bully boys, blow.

And what do you think we had for breakfast?
Blow, boys, blow.
The starboard side of an old sou'wester.
Blow, boys, bully boys, blow.

Then what do you think we had for dinner?
Blow, boys, blow.
Old haddock guts and vile shark's liver.
Blow, boys, bully boys, blow.

Now can you guess what we had for supper
Blow, boys, blow.
We had strong salt junk and weak tea water.
Blow, boys, bully boys, blow.

Then blow us fair today and tomorrow
Blow, boys, blow.
Blow us home without no sorrow.
Blow, boys, bully boys, blow.

Blow us steady and without much labour
Blow, boys, blow.

And so, the merriment went into the balmy night naming as many of the crew as came to mind with much jocularity and all had fond memories of the day we crossed the line.

The next day with the morning watch still feeling the worst after their evening's festivities, we picked up the edge of the Southeast Trade Winds and after a few days sailed around the headland of the Brazilian city of Salvador, also known as São Salvador da Bahia de Todos os Santos[29] and into the beautiful wide Bay of All Saints. This bay was reported to be one of the best whale breeding areas in this part of the world and indeed, after we had replenished our coal and general stores, we had just departed two days later when we sighted a large pod of whales just offshore.

It was here that we chanced upon an interesting feature of our new technology. Excited by the prospect of catching our first whale, and with the winds being very light and from an inopportune direction, we decided to hunt the whales using our engine alone. With all of our sails furled and our engine at full steam we headed out after the pod. Unfortunately, they easily became alarmed and dived deeply. At no time were we able to close in on the pod. It

---

[28] Adapted from an old New Bedford whaling halyard song.
[29] Portuguese: *'Saint Savior from the Bay of All Saints'*

soon became very obvious that it was the sound of our engine which had scared the whales. Moreover, our engine could not give us the speed to come up to the whales quick enough to launch our boats. From now on, we would have to hunt the whale in the old manner with the silence which only sail can give and by stealth. Our auxiliary engine would have to be used for our general transport at times when our sails could not be used. I remembered a casual conversation with our good friend Peder Andersen whilst be lunched in Bergen about the future of whaling. He had mentioned that a friend of his Sven Foyn, who was also in shipping, had once expressed a view that one day the great whale would be hunted offshore using small, fast, steam-powered whale hunting ships which would have a harpoon-firing gun which would kill a whale with one shot. Father had laughed at such a proposal, as whaling, to him, was an honourable profession requiring the wits and ability of the whaler alone against the great beast in its own territory. Personally, I thought that such hunting was more of an efficient killing business rather than a noble profession. I must confess that even wonderful vessels such as the *Australis* might push these beautiful animals into extinction. Indeed, we were troubled when our chandler at São Salvador da Baha, Senhor Gonçalves lamented that the whaling trade had recently diminished in local waters due to the recent incursions of other Yankee whalers.

And so, with somewhat of a heavy heart we continued our voyage south, down along the coastline of Brazil, past the port of Montevideo, which was being blockaded by the

British and so inaccessible to us for further replenishment of our stores. As we still had enough coal, water and stores on board to last for a considerable time, we charted a course due south for the Falkland Islands.

Suddenly there was a call from the masthead. "Whale ho! Board on the port quarter!"

"How far?" I called.

"She'm be about two cables[30], zur! She broaches!" came the reply.

"Bring her about, helmsman. All boats away!" I called. This brought the crew into a well-trained fever of activity. Men ran to their allotted tasks with good humour and laughter. After our long voyage this was the closest we had come to a surfaced whale so the men looked forward to the hunt. In a thrice the starboard gun'le was lowered, the boats' davits were put into place and the men began the task of lowering our six whale boats over the side. As each boat went over the side, the harpooner then the rest of the crew jumped down into the whaler. Soon all boats were away, heading for the last sighting of the whale.

As Captain, I stayed on board as it was my father's wish that I should do so. From the top of the aft deckhouse I

---

[30] A cable is nautical term for length as well as referring to ropes etc. It is about 600 feet with 10 cables making up one nautical mile. A cable is also about 183 metres.

watched the drama unfold as first one harpoon and then another was sunk deep within our quarry. Within a few hours, the whale tired and then it was that the harpooner, Miantumi of boat number four, went aft and changed places with the captain of the boat, boatheader Daniel Rawlinson another native American, who then carried his lance forward and plunged it into the whale's heart. As the whaleboat backed off we watched the awesome spectacle of the death of the whale. The great beast swam in a flurry of ever smaller circles until the whale beat the water with its tail, shuddered and turned fin out and died. Now the dead whale was towed back to the ship and secured with heavy chains to our starboard side below the platform of the lowered gun'le. The other boats joined the victorious boat which had now rowed around the port side, ready to be raised aboard. As they came on board, Miantumi and Rawlinson sang the death song of the Narragansett people as penance and tribute to the whale they had killed. Few whalermen were not moved by the death of their victims and many a good Quaker from New Bedford would offer a prayer that night for the life of the great whale and the safety of the men who hunted her.

There now began the usual pitch of activity associated with the cutting up and processing of the whale. This had to be done quickly as the blood from the dead whale and the other pieces thrown overboard soon attracted the sharks. Whilst I had missed the thrill of the hunt, it was my prerogative as Captain to assist in this process by taking some target practice at some of the sharks as they came in for their feeding. Accordingly, I fetched one of the rifles from the arms chest in my cabin and a box of mini ball cartridges. I sat well out on the roof of the foc'sle cabin and found that I had a good arc of fire well away from my working crew. It was more a sport than a practical prevention as there were sharks aplenty and the crew worked feverously to cut away the useful portions of our catch before hauling them on board. The crew was now divided into two watches, each worked six-hour shifts, day and night, until the job was done.

The cutting crew leapt down onto the floating carcass to begin the process of stripping off the blubber, a thick layer of fat, with the various flensing tools used to peel off strips which were then hooked onto lines and hauled aboard. These long strips or 'blanket pieces' were then cut up on deck into smaller 'horse pieces' and Bible leaves, so-called because they resembled books. It was brutal and dangerous work as the large quantity of blood on the deck and carcass made the surfaces extremely slippery and they had to be constantly washed down to prevent men from slipping overboard to the sharks below. Moreover, as the larger pieces of blubber being hauled on board could weigh up to a ton, it was wise for every man on deck to be vigilant.

On deck, the fires in the brick furnaces below the try pots had been lit and stoked up. The smaller Bible leaves of blubber were then tossed into the iron pots and cooked until the oil was rendered from the blubber. This was run off into vats, cooled and then placed in our casks then rolled down ramps to be stored in the hold of the ship. Our whale was a young humpback[31] and would give us a few good barrels of oil but its baleen[32] was usually considered useless. The next morning, having cleared up the deck by casting the remains of our catch overboard, we set sail. We continued our voyage south to the Falkland Islands, sailing around to the leeward side of the eastern island to Blanco Bay where we negotiated the narrows into the harbour of Port Stanley and anchored opposite the settlement. This we found to be a wind-swept place with only a few stone buildings and fewer people who had migrated here from other parts of the island and Britain only a few years before our arrival. The countryside beyond the settlement appears to be of a hilly, heathlands with grass and a few low shrubs with sheep being the main product of the island. There is some controversy about these islands as the Argentinians claim them also; being the 'birth right' as it were following their independence from Spain. They claim that these islands which they call Islas Malvinas had been given to them by the French in the 18th century but the islands have often been deserted, claimed and reclaimed for many years. Now the British have only recently declared them a Crown Colony.

---

[31] *Megaptera novaeangliae* which grows up to about 15 metres in length and weighs up to 50 tons and humps its back when it dives.

[32] Baleen whales have long strips, which hang from the roofs of their mouths, which they use to strain out krill from sea water. This was used in a variety of nineteenth-century products such as in whips carriage springs; corset stays and other applications for which plastic or steel would now be used.

We stayed at Port Stanley for a few days, reorganising the products of our first catch and bartering with the local crofters[33] for meat and other food supplies. In the town there were limited resources although some of the local store-owners had imported some chandlery items and timber for the replenishment of passing ships like ours. Port Stanley was a useful base for our whaling operations south of the islands. The charts promised an open stretch of water to the south east which should be an excellent hunting ground for some of the larger whales. As we sailed further south, we found however, a violent ocean filled with icebergs, both large and small, high winds and a strong westerly current. We had not sailed more than three days before we encountered pack ice as far as our lookout could see. During this time of several weeks we had taken only one other whale, a juvenile blue[34] before retreating once more to Port Stanley. This area did not bode well for good whaling, so in consultation with Mr Warren and my other officers, we put it to the crew that we should try our luck further west beyond what Bransfield[35] had called the Trinity Peninsula.

---

[33] A crofter is one who has tenure and use of the land, typically as a tenant sheep farmer.
[34] The blue whale (*Balaenoptera musculus*) is a baleen whale up to 29.9 metres (98 ft) in length and with a maximum recorded weight of 173 tonnes (190 short tons) and is the largest animal known to have ever existed. As with other baleen whales, its diet consists almost exclusively of small crustaceans known as krill which it filters out using its baleen - bristles of keratin (as in human fingernails and hair) arranged in plates across the upper jaw of the whale.

[35] Edward Bransfield (1785 – 1852) was an Irish sailor who rose to become an officer in the British Royal Navy, serving as a master on several ships. He is noted for exploring and charting parts of Antarctica, sighting what he called Trinity Land in January 1820, the northern most part of the Antarctic Peninsula.

Chapter Seven
Lands of Fire and Ice

Latitude 62°58' 37" South; Longitude 60° 39' 00" West
30ºF, high winds 30 knots from the West

On the next day, which was fine with a light nor'easter blowing, we left Blanc Bay under steam. Rounding Cape Pembroke, we set all sail to head southwest.

We had set our course slightly to the south of southwest so that we would give good clearance to Cape San Juan, the eastern most tip of Isla de los Estados, which in English is also called Staten Island. This land lies off the coast of Tierra del Fuego and belongs to the Argentine. In such as unpredictable sea, it was thought that we should give this land a wide berth rather than use the narrow le Maire Straits which separate the island from the mainland by only sixteen nautical miles[1].

Remarkably for such a sea noted for its storms, we had good sailing and passed the Cape on our starboard beam just as the sun was setting in the Second Dog Watch[2]. We were now entering the Drake Passage sailing in the wrong direction to those who braved this passage past Cape Horn.

The Drake Passage is that narrow strait which lies between the tip of South America and the Antarctica Peninsula. To

---

[1] Approximately 29 kilometres.
[2] The Second Dog Watch consists of a two-hour ship from 4 pm to 6 pm.

be more precise, it is that stretch of sea between Cape Horn, the southernmost tip of Horn Island lying off the end of Tierra del Fuego and the South Shetland Islands which lie off the coast of the Antarctic Peninsula. It is about 430 nautical miles wide[3] but notorious for its storms and the difficulty in which to manoeuvre a square-rigged ship.

For a landsman, such a distance seems like a wide berth, but the Drake Passage is well known for its unfavourable winds, currents and storms. The prevailing winds here are the Furious Fifties because the Passage is at fifty degrees south latitude. To the north in the open ocean of the Pacific, are the more famous Roaring Forties. These fast-flowing winds blow from the east and are funnelled into the narrow Drake Passage with the Andes to the north and their extension along the Antarctic Peninsula to the south. This also causes a strong eastward-flowing current called the Antarctic Circumpolar Current which is particularly strong in the relatively shallow waters of the Passage.

So far, we had been lucky. On the third day out of Port Stanley we encountered a backing of the eastward current and a sudden drop in the winds. I awoke and heard the three bells of the Morning Watch[4]. There was something unusual about the ship which slowly entered my sleepy mind. No longer was there the sound of water rushing below the hull and the occasional slap of a contrary wave,

---

[3] About 800 kilometres
[4] About 5:30 am

but a silence most disturbing. The ship seemed to be almost motionless but with a slight wallowing movement. I quickly dressed and went up on deck. Opening the cabin door, I was presented with a thick grey fog. I could just make out the stoic form of the helmsman at the wheel and the gun'les on the starboard side. The sea was like glass, oily and slightly heaving like the back of some huge, stricken whale. From out of the dense fog Caleb Warren, the First Mate appeared like some apparition.

"It's a bad day for sailing, Cap'n Jamie" his pipe giving an eerie red glow at every puff.

"Aye, it looks that way, Mr Warren. We must sound our fog horn if you please for their may be other ships in this pea-soup".

The first mate turned to the quartermaster's mate who stood by the helmsman and now pulled on a line which hung from the roof of the small cabin.

Three long blasts issued from the ships steam siren on the side of the funnel. This was something new for the crew who had been raised on the melancholy sound of a hand-cranked fog horn which sounded not unlike the lowing of cattle.

"Aye. It's a strange morning, alright Cap'n. I was taking to one of the watch earlier – old Seth Rowlings – you know the man, Captain Jamie. He's the old seaman with the gold earring. He's an old Cape Horner who has sailed these waters many times. He was telling me that the waters here abouts have a stormy reputation, but at times such a calm can come upon a ship when the wind backs and the warm air from the north comes down over the colder waters from the Antarctic. We must be close to the edge of the Antarctic Convergence[5] and this pea-souper is the result."

"I think that you are right, Mr Warren" I replied. "When the fog lifts, I shall try to shoot the sun[6] to get our bearings, but I fear that the Drake Passage will live up to its reputation later in the day.

True enough, by the end of the Morning Watch, the fog had lifted and the wind had backed[7] from the slight sou 'easterly of the night into a fresh breeze from the south west.

With a few short hours, the winds had changed and confirmed the Drake Passage's bad reputation. Mr Warren gave orders for all the sails to be hauled up except reefed[8]

---

[5] This is the natural boundary varying in latitude seasonally, where cold, northward-flowing Antarctic waters meet and sink below the relatively warmer waters of the subantarctic.

[6] Sighting the sun using the sextant at noon and thus getting the ship's latitude or angular bearing from the Equator. Using the ship's chronometer or clock, the distance from the Prime Meridian at Greenwich would also give the ship's longitude and thus a complete bearing or position.

[7] Backing— according to general internationally accepted usage, this is a change in wind direction in an anticlockwise sense (e.g., south to southeast to east) in either hemisphere of the Earth; the opposite of veering.

[8] Reefing sails – part of the sail is hauled up and lashed to the spars so that the sail area is reduced.

topsails, the flying jib and the spanker. Under this set of canvas, we would be able to more favourably tack into the strong wind.

Gradually the wind became strong and more from the west, our desired direction. Tacking became a regular and arduous task for all of our watches were needed on the halyards as we turned across the wind first to the southwest and then back across towards the northwest. In this fashion we were able to bear to windward at only one to two knots.

I went to the brass speaking tube near the helm which led down into the engine room and ordered Mr Dunsmuir to raise full steam in our engine.
"Och aye, it's abit time tae gie thes ship movin!" came the laconic reply.

By now the sea was running with waves about twenty[9] feet high and the wind at Force 9[10]. The sea was also in a confused state as the swell from our previous winds was still coming from the southeast. The topsail fluttered alarmingly on the almost bare mast whose head swung wildly in a figure-of-eight. One moment we were on a wave crest and could see a vast mass of surging grey waves topped with white water which crashed down their swirling slopes. The next moment we were down in a deep trough, surrounded by walls of fiercely dark water with our

---

[9] About 6.5 metres

[10] Force 9 on the Beaufort Scale means that the winds were at a severe gale and blowing at about 80 kilometres per hour with waves up to 10 metres high.

little ship struggling to climb up the next wave. It is difficult to describe the awe and fear which comes to even the most seasoned sailor in a storm at sea. We had the best ship that has ever been built - for Peder Andersen has built her to withstand the stormiest seas of the North Atlantic and then some – but here and now, in the middle of the stormiest passage of the world, we all felt the full power of an angry sea.

Lifelines had been rigged along the inner deck as white water regularly came over the gun'les. No man was able to move unless he was attached to one of these lines. All deck cargo, especially the try pots and boats had been doubly lashed and two hands manned the wheel.

We struggled this way for four days, making very little headway. Below decks there was chaos in the crew's mess in the foc'sle which rose and fell at an alarming rate. Personal items flew everywhere and any man attempting to move was thrown about the cabin. Lars, the big carpenter, did his best to shore up any leaks in the lower hull and to secure any part of the ship which could freely move but men were still thrown across the foc'sle or were hit by falling objects so that many a bloody face or hand became a common sight. Heavily clothed in their oilskins, the crew battled to keep the ship on its westward course into the teeth of the gale. On that night I had retired to my cabin and teetered back and forth along the swaying deck trying to undress for bed. Finally, I gave up and slumped back into the bunk having only just succeeding in taking off my sea boots and heavy coat. Suddenly, a rogue wave hit our gallant ship and I was thrown bodily out of the bunk and across the cabin, hitting the far bulkhead with a sudden force. I crawled back to the bunk and despite being fully clothed, pulled the counterpane up to my chin and forcefully tucked its edges in and under the mattress. Now enclosed in my strong cacoon, I would try to sleep. But to no avail.

The next morning the storm had not abated so with our topsails in tatters, we reluctantly decided to go about and end our quest to hunt the whale in the great Southern Ocean west of Cape Horn. Instead we would go to the South Shetland Islands, a place known to have sizeable whale populations, but also one sometimes frequented by other whalers.

Not able to find our position by using the sun, we estimated our position by dead-reckoning[11] to be well past the tip of South America. There was no point in turning northward along the coast of Chile as whaling had been a well-established trade in those waters, so we head on a course southeast towards the Antarctic Peninsula.

The South Shetland Islands form a long chain of islands running parallel to the greater Antarctic Peninsula starting from its northern-most tip, the Trinity Peninsula. As such,

---

[11] A very rough estimate of position from the last know sun-sighting using time and speed to estimate distance travelled and the compass bearings taken over that time.

and with the wind now behind us, this would be a dangerous lee shore[12].

These islands had been discovered only some forty years previously by Captain William Smith of *The Williams* whilst carrying cargo from Buenos Aires in Brazil to Valparaíso in Chile. He also had attempted to sail westward past the Horn but had taken a more southerly course than we had taken, in doing so he had discovered these islands which he had named in honour of the Shetland Islands north of Scotland.

Now we were running before the wind and our speed increased to six knots. The topmen were able to take down our tattered topsails to fit a new set so now we were able to run with a modest set of canvas much to the chagrin of our Scotch Engineer who swore that his engine would have eventually beaten the gales. I said nothing against this, even though I had heard incidentally that he had been running his engine at full steam.

In the evening of the fourth day after going about we heard the long-awaited cry from aloft:

"Land-ho on the starboard bow!" We all rushed to the bow and I grabbed my glass[13] as I ran from the cabin. There, in

---

[12] Lee – the direction away from the wind as opposed to 'windward' which is towards the wind. A lee shore is one towards which a ship is being blown and is thus considered a potential danger.
[13] Telescope

front of the ship at about a league[14] distant was an island; generally low but with a high peak on its northern side. As the sun was setting and there were several large icebergs between us and land, I decided to hove-to[15] for the night rather than sail in the darkness on a lee shore.

"Back the mains'ls and haul up all tops'ls" cried Mr Warren through his speaking trumpet. The crew raced aloft to furl the topsails whilst the ship was slowed down with the mains. Soon they had all sails furled and the spanker reefed just in case we needed some manoeuvring. There was a slight drift towards the shore so a sea-anchor was thrown out. The crew stood down to night routine but an extra watch was posted in case we encountered ice during the night.

I was awoken at dawn by Thomas, our young steward and trainee seaman with a cup of good black coffee.

"Good morning to you sir. It'll be a fine morning I'm thinking." He said with a slight Irish brogue as Thomas Dillan hailed from Limerick in Eire, he had signed on to the *Australis* as a 14-year-old orphan having made his way across the Atlantic. I sat up in my bunk and was gratified to see a faint glimmer of sunlight coming through the port.

---

[14] League – a unit of distance used on the sea and one league is approximately three nautical miles or about 5.6 kilometres.

[15] Hove to - is a way of slowing a sailboat's forward progress, as well as fixing the helm and sail positions so that the boat does not have to be steered.

"Thank'ee, Thomas." I replied as I jumped out of my bunk, dressed and went out on deck. There was some sun low on the eastern horizon which stood a little off our starboard beam as the current had turned the ship slightly to the north. Our land was now much closer and off our port beam was a huge iceberg not too distant.

Icebergs were not unknown to the crew as these ice mountains often drift down the east coast of Canada and sometimes into American waters. Moreover, hunting the whale in the North Atlantic always had some peril of such monsters. This berg was bigger than most I had encountered. It was far longer than our ship and higher than our mast. With vertical sides with icy overhangs it was totally white with new snow on top but gradually became a beautiful, translucent pale blue colour near the water's edge. The morning sun glinted red on one side; the overall effect was most inspiring.

"Icebergs form off the ends of glaciers." I remarked to young Thomas who had come up to the gun'le by my side. This was his first time into a land of ice so he was totally awestruck by the size of the iceberg now in front of us.

"They break off, or 'calve' when the glacier – that's a large mass of ice on shore – when it meets to the sea."

"Why do they float so, sir?" the boy asked.

Our first iceberg with the whaler far right

Into the Gerlache Strait

"Well, Thomas," I replied, "the ice is freshwater so it floats on the sea which is heavier like, but most of it is below the water level and it may widen out so we must keep a goodly berth from her."

"See, it is mostly white with snow and blue ice below the water." I said, pointing to the berg. "This and its size mean that it is only a young iceberg – probably coming from the mainland not too far away, but they do drift for long distances. As they age, they become smaller as some snow melts or compacts and they become more icy and some older ones are almost clear ice but no bigger than our ship's boats. There are even green icebergs with marine plant growths under their ice and brown ones which have earth and rock within them."

Mister Warren came up with a grin on his battered face. "Well now, Captain Jamie," he said. "Joseph was able to take a fix on Acrux[16] during First Watch with a break in the cloud and reckons that we're about Latitude 62° South; and Longitude 60° West."

"Excellent, Mr Warren. Give Mr Turling my sincere compliments for his quick thinking and able navigation. So, let us consult the chart."

---

[16] Acrux or Alpha Crucis is the brightest star in the constellation of the Southern Cross, the most prominent star pattern in high southern latitudes. Joseph Turling is the second mate of the *Australis* and had sailed the southern hemisphere many times.

In the navigation cabin we took down a well-worn chart that father had obtained from the British Naval survey of the area of 1829. Using the parallel ruler were plotted our approximate position on the chart.

"Why!" I exclaimed. "That land ahead must be Nathanial Palmer's Deception Island."

"Aye, it lies at 62°58' 37" South; Longitude 60° 39' 00" West." said Caleb Warren, measuring the angles off the chart. "It shows a circular harbour in its midst with a narrow entrance on its eastern side. A good place to catch up on few repairs, I'm a thinkin'."

"Yes, I recall now from reading Palmer's logbook, a copy of which father had obtained, that it was once a large volcano that blew to pieces leaving a large hole which filled with the sea through this narrow entrance. Look! That entrance is called Neptune's Bellows so it would be wise, I think to use our engine through the narrows."

"To be certain, Cap'n Jamie," replied the first mate.
"You can see that the entrance is not that simple. There be a rock – marked as 'Raven's Rock with only a little over one and a half fathoms[17]."

We sailed up under canvas as the wind was still blowing at about thirty knots and rounded the southern edge of the

---

[17] Fathom – unit of depth of about 1.8 metres.

island until we could see the entrance. Indeed, the island lived up to its name as Deception Island. Nathaniel Palmer, the whaler, who had visited the island in the sloop *Hero* in 1820, had thought it to be just another rocky island covered in ice and snow. Sailing through the opening he called Neptune's Bellows, on account of the strong winds blowing through it, he found himself coming into a large, circular stretch of water which filled the entire centre of the island leaving only a narrow circle of mountains around its edge.

With our engine running and all sails furled, we took the *Australis* over close to the starboard or northern side of the entrance. The cliffs were impressive - being of that dark red and black colour associated with some of the volcanic islands of the Canaries which I had visited as a boy. These cliffs, however rose vertically from the sea and were capped with ice and new snow. Even on the lee of the island, our entrance was rough. Close on our starboard beam, the black cliffs rose vertically as a series of jagged spires but far over on our port beam the tall, brown, snow-capped cliffs came down to the sea as a long, steep slope of broken brown rock. The westerly winds blew over the distant ridge and pushed long rollers of white-capped waves against our bow. The harbour itself was incredible! In the far distance, at several leagues, was a steep-sided ridge which ran right around the near circular harbour. Here and there were small glaciers running down through narrow valleys of dark brown rock and the entire circular rim was covered in snow and ice.

Into Neptune's Bellows

The anchorage inside Deception Island

Having entered the harbour under steam, we were able to make a short tour of the rocky shore. In most places the steep, rocky slopes came right down to the water's edge but in a few places, there were long, flat arms of compacted brown soil and rock which stretched out into the water like long, broad fingers. The lead was heaved and the depth was uniformly found to exceed its length of fifty fathoms. Coming up to the entrance again we saw that there was a small circular bay opening out before the northern-most headland. We slowly steamed into this bay and found that the depth had come up as a narrow ledge at about twenty fathoms – enough for us to anchor.

Not far from the shore, we let out the anchor and let the ship settle into the wind that was blowing across the mouth of the bay. By the time the boat stopped moving we were down to about 2 fathoms close inshore. It being a low tide, we though that this was sufficient for a safe anchorage. The wind was blowing 20 knots through the anchorage and the temperature was warmer than I had expected at just a few degrees below freezing.

Consulting the earlier charts and some whaling journals which father had collected, my suspicions were confirmed that Deception Island was volcanic. A report from the log of the whaler *Ohio*, which had referred to 'flames appearing on the southern shore'. Deception Island was then the remains of an exploded volcano with its central harbour being but the flooded centre or caldera, which had formed when the interior of the volcano had collapsed. Surveying those parts of the southern and western shores which I could see from the top of the deckhouse with my spyglass, I perceived some faint tendrils of steam issuing from small vents here and there. The long, flat fingers of land then had been more recent lava flows which had hardened.

My exploration into the island's Natural History was confirmed when Caleb Warren and I led a small party ashore onto the black sandy beach just opposite our ship. Jumping ashore, I found to my surprise that the wet sand was indeed warm and it took some of the men by surprise as well. As the air temperature was now well-below freezing, being able to stand in warm water with a strong and cold wind whipping the upper part of the body, even through our good sea clothing, was a strange experience. It did not take the men too long to have hollowed out a large indentation in the beach which thus formed a wide warm-water pool. With suitable encouragement, several of them quickly stripped off their clothing and immersed themselves bodily below the warm water. There was much laughter on the beach and from the ship where their shipmates had observed this spontaneous frivolity. Soon, small parties of seamen where coming ashore to engage in their own hot water baths along the beach.

We spent the next two weeks here at our new harbour. Men were posted on the rocky headland which overlooked the broad strait to the east, but that was an unpopular posting with little cover from the icy winds and almost a mile from our camp. Occasionally a whale would be sighted and a man would come scrambling down the brown scree slope to tell us so. There would be a mad dash for the two boats we had ashore and a fast row out to the *Australis*. Mr Dunsmuir was not happy with this mode of whaling as he was obliged to keep steam up on his boiler so that we could get underway quickly. This meant that his stokers would have to keep the pressure up over all daytime watches.

The anchor would be raised and we would steam out after the whale. This took considerable time and so more likely as not, the whale had long since passed. In our time at Deception Island we took only one small Humpback whale.

On this our second last day at the island, I was onboard and leaning over the railing at the end of the morning watch and in a mood of deep melancholy. The cloud had come down over the peaks of the island and the sea was a listless grey. Mr Warren was also onboard and came on deck.
"Morning to you, Cap'n Jamie", he said.

"Good morning to you also, Mr Warren." I replied without looking up but continuing to lean on the gun'le and stare across the water towards the sea. He must have sensed my feelings – he had been with the family for many years and knew me since I was a small boy.

"It's a grey old day, Jaimie. Are ye not well?" he enquired.

I looked up and turned around to face him. "Ah, no! Nothing of great consequence, Caleb. It is just the depressing nature of our voyage so far. This is a great place for a base to catch the whale, but our ship is too big to get out when they come and it is a long and dangerous pull in our whale boats to hunt from here."

He came to my side and rested his arms on the gun'le and looked into my eyes "Aye, it is that. I hear that they are making small, fast steamers in Norway that come out of their bays and hunt the whale in the open sea. Perhaps they would be better suited for our present camp?"

"Yes, so I have heard. There is a whaler called Sven Foyn who has suggested that one day he may build a small steamer which hunts whales from the shores of Norway. They would be fast in most weathers and could be armed with a gun that can shoot a harpoon a long way. Perhaps this is the new way our trade is heading and our way of hunting the whale in the open sea will become only something of the past."

"Ah, well, Cap'n Jamie. Perhaps that might be so, but whales are not stupid enough to travel inshore where they can be hunted. Our old friends of the Inuit and the Narragansett tribes will tell you that. They gave up their traditional hunting in their long canoes after we took to whaling in bigger ships. Mr Foyn will soon run out of whales along his shore too in time."

"It is more than that, Caleb." I replied. "We have come a long way to get whales because there are now few in home waters. Are we hunting them to extinction? Can we not do without hunting these magnificent creatures?"

"Well, now Cap'n Jamie. That I wouldn't know. I've been a whalerman since I was a boy and I only know this trade. But I do know that lot's o' people on the shore depend upon our work, an' there's a ready market for the riches given to us by the whale. Why, apart from the oil and grease which lights our lamps and makes our candles, there's the bone that makes buttons and stuff for the ladies. And meat of course. Aye. The whale is needed more than ever. Never you fear that!"

"Aye. I guess that you are right in your assessment of our trade, Mr Warren." I replied. "But it seems like our trade will one day cease to be useful. Perhaps we will find other things to replace the bounty given to us by these magnificent creatures when they cease to swim in their oceans."

Caleb Warren, being much older and wiser than I changed the subject of our sombre conversation by taking a step back from the side of the ship and looking out past me and into the bay. "Well, now. That is might be, Cap'n Jamie, but where do we go from here?"

I stood back from the railing and motioned him to follow me into the chart room.
"Let us go and find some good water to go a'whaling," I said with as much cheer as I could muster.

I had the old Royal Navy chart already on the chart table, unrolled it and place the dividers and parallel rule on its edges to stop it curling.

"Look'ee here. Mr Warren!" I said pointing to the open water southwest of our island. "Here is shown open water, between Low Island and Trinity Island, in what they called the Bransfield Strait[18]. That is a good piece of open water to look for our elusive whale. Are all the repairs complete, Mr Warren?"

"Aye, Sir. They finished fishing[19] our split fore topmast just this mornin' and by all appearances we should be ready to sail."

---

[18] is a body of water about 100 kilometres wide extending for 500 km in a general northeast – southwest direction between the South Shetland Islands and the Antarctic Peninsula. The strait was named in about 1825 by James Weddell, Master, Royal Navy, for Edward Bransfield, Master, RN, who charted the South Shetland Islands in 1820.

[19] To fish a mast, or yard, is to fasten a piece of timber, or plank, (by way of splinter) to the mast or yard, to strengthen it; this piece or plank is called a fish.

Chapter Eight
Another Ship

Latitude 64°24' 22" South; Longitude 62° 19' 47" West
25ºF, high winds 20 knots from the West

The next morning, all things in the ship and onshore having been squared-away, we left our anchorage in Deception Island and headed out through Neptune's Bellows and into the Bransfield Strait under steam.

Outside we found the wind blowing as a fresh breeze from the Northwest. Sheltered in the chartroom, the air temperature was a balmy twenty-five degrees but outside, the wind dropped the temperature to a bracing -6 degrees Fahrenheit. Accordingly, we stopped the engine and hoisted only our top'sls and gibs and set out course sou'west.

The sea carried moderate swells with a little foam and spray into the dull, grey air above. The sky was uniformly covered in a low, light grey cloud but visibility was good. The crew went about their morning tasks with some cheer now that we were again under sail and heading into new waters. The days at Deception Island had been a good respite from our stormy introduction to this grey continent, but the lack of activity and failure to sight any whales had brought about an intense feeling of ennui amongst us all. We were all glad of the bracing wind and a moderate sea clear of ice.

It was well into the Second Dog Watch[1] and the sun still gave some faint illumination through the heavy overcast. In these latitudes, like their counterpart in the Northern hemisphere, the sun in summer usually does not dip below the horizon until almost midnight. I was sitting in the charthouse checking our location by dead reckoning on our course to a safe anchorage on the lee shore of a large island[2] shown on Nathaniel Palmer's chart of thirty years ago. Suddenly there was the traditional cry of "Whale Ho!". But it came not from the masthead as was expected but just outside the cabin at the deck level. Dropping my dividers, I rushed out on deck to see our cabin boy Thomas Dillon, excited and with arm outstretched over the port gun'le.

"Look'ee, Cap'n, a whale!" he cried. I followed his arm and saw a broad wave rapidly approaching the ship less than a cable's[3] length away. It was a small Humpback whale and its nebulous spume formed a thin mist over its passage towards the ship.

By now many of the crew had run to the side of the ship and were wildly shouting at each other over the wind.

---

[1] The Dog Watches are only of 2 hours duration so as to break up the pattern of the other watches. The First Dog Watch starts at 4 pm and the Second at 6 pm. The term has an obscure meaning but some say it is a shortening of the term to "dodge the watch" as the sailors doing it only do two hours not four.

[2] Later named Brabant Island in 1887 by a Belgium expedition after a province of that country.

[3] A cable is an old unit of length equal to one tenth of a nautical mile. Depending upon how it is converted, a cable length can be anywhere from 169 to 220 metres.

"She'm goin' ta ram us!" shouted Isaac Townley, one of our foretopman[4], who had often recounted the story of the ill-fated *Essex*, whaler which had been rammed and suck by a whale in 1820.

"Calm your fears, Isaac!" I said. This is a small humpback, not a great sperm whale." And at this our whale arched its back and its fluke raised high in the air as it dived below our keel.

The men all ran to the other side of the ship and laughed as they wished our curious visitor a safe journey.

"Shall we go after her. Cap'n?" said Isaac Townley.

"No, she'll be too far away by the time we lower our boats. And besides, I am not too sure of how much light we have left in these latitudes."

"Back to your watch, men!" cried Joseph Turling our second mate, and the ship once more resumed its silent passage.

I had not ever thought about the sounds of our passage further south. Of course, in a good wind there are always a variety of sounds in a ship under sail: the rhythmic luffing of a clew of a poorly adjusted sail[5]; the rattling of some

---

[4] A sailor whose job it is to handle the sails in the upper foremast (forward mast).
[5] This is the shaking of the lower ends (clews) of a square sail.

other line of sheet against the rigging; the smooth hiss of the water flowing beneath the bow; and the usual creaks and groans of stressed timbers. Now there was almost absolute silence. The wind had dropped and was behind us. The sea had become flatter and very air was still. It was that time of day when the crew would have retired to their night duties; those on watch to stand silently around the deck or in the rigging looking for ice or whales, the helmsman silently at the wheel intent on the lubber line moving slightly back and forth in the dim glow of the binnacle lamp. The rest of the crew not on watch would have retired to the Foc'sle for a little warm shelter, some food and perhaps some scant sleep before they are woken for their turn on watch.

I stood quietly at the ship's side and looked out over the dim, grey seascape that stretched out to the infinity of rock, snow and ice beyond. There were a few small ice floes now floating past but they were of little consequence. I walked over to the port side and saw the faint shapeless mass of land distant in the fine mist which was now settling on the silent sea. There was no living thing in sight. Even the few sea birds which often followed the ship had gone to whatever roost they could find in this inhospitable land. Melancholy swept over me and I thought that perhaps our task ahead was to be as fruitless as our days on Deception Island. "Oh, well," I thought, "tomorrow may bring better tidings" and took my evening stroll around the deck. We had now closed up to the eastern shore of this big island

and at some distance south since we had entered the strait[6] between it and the mainland. As our leadsman up at the bow had called a series of depths suggesting that the sea floor was beginning to shoal, I gave orders for the *Australis* to be brought into the wind and the anchor dropped for the short night. All being well and everything shipshape, I too retired to my cabin as the sea mist rolled over the ship.

To my surprise, the dim light of dawn to our east presented a far from dismal scene. There was still a layer of cloud over the entire sky but it was now much higher and the sea mist had cleared. Visibility was good but now we could see a few more ice floes drifting slowly in the open strait. Most of this drift ice ranged from about ten yards or more across to others which were much smaller. Generally, they were flat on top and very white; the youngest floes being of this colour and composed of compacted snow on top and hard, blue ice below. Others had rounded or elliptical coverings of snow or were taller and had been eroded by the wind into grotesque spires and ridges. These we thought had been the remains of smaller icebergs which had broken off the main glaciers and fast ice around the island and mainland shores. A few smaller and older floes were almost clear and were simply lumps of ice drifting past the ship and occasionally bumping into our strengthened hull. There was some laughter over on the port side of the ship where our cook, Jacob Simmons and his crew had managed

---

[6] Now called the Gerlache Strait which was named by Lt. Adrien de Gerlache, who explored the strait in January and February 1898, naming it for the expedition ship *Belgica* but later it was renamed after its discoverer.

to lasso one of these glassy rafts and was now hauling it aboard using tackle from the boom of the foremast. It measured several yards long and was perfectly clear. "This'll be nice chopped up in our whiskey", he cried.

Things were looking much better than my previous night of melancholy. There was plenty of open sea room to our east and the mountainous island nearby was good protection from the strong, prevailing westerly winds. Standing on the roof of the aft deckhouse with a big mug of fresh coffee from Jacob's galley, I felt much more content. The wind had dropped to only the occasional light airs and I had time to take a closer look at this harsh land. Away on the port side I saw a darkened shape on the intense white of one of the larger floes. I retrieved my glass from the chartroom and focussed the lens. The shape proved to be a seal. A little longer than a man, it had a uniformly grey, smooth coat and a handsome face with big whiskers. I went into the chartroom and consulted the many diaries which had details of the wildlife of these waters been made by some of the early whalers. There it was! A nicely-drawn sketch of my seal. It was a Weddell seal, or *Leptonychotes weddellii*, named after the British sea captain James Weddell who had charted these waters in the 1820s. We were now closer into land than previous, save our short stay on Deception which seemed to be barren of life. Seals, penguins and other birds soon became obvious once we looked for them. Our cook had already found that the sea was full of a great variety of fish and our leadsman had often found evidence of bottom-dwelling life on the end of his lead and tallow line.

Late in the First Dog Watch, we came into a large bay surrounded by two massive glaciers on most of its shore and a rocky bluff with a long snow slope at its furthest point. The glaciers came down to the water's edge and ended abruptly in tall, crinkled and jagged cliffs of blue ice. There was a semicircle of broken sea ice around the shore on the far side but generally the bay afforded a good anchorage with open water so I decided to anchor here for the night. There was still plenty of daylight left so I ordered that two boats should be launched to inspect the rocky headland and possibly secure some more ice for our freshwater supplies. One of our foretopmen had seen a dark, rocky mass high up on the snow slope which he though may be a penguin rookery and this too, was worth investigating.

Our two boats were lowered and I commanded one and Mr Warren our First Mate commanded the other. Our Second Mate, Joseph Turling was left in command of the ship. We rowed directly across the bay towards the rocky headland, for to skirt around the shoreline below the glaciers would be a foolhardy thing to do for occasionally a large part of the face of one of the glaciers would break off with a loud crack like the report of a gun and slide gracefully down into the cold grey waters of the bay.

It was a good half an hour or more until we reached the broken ice pack which surrounded the shore below the rocky headland. With some difficulty we managed to push our two small boats through the broken ice, Taumalolo, our giant Pacific Islander being very useful at pushing the large, flat slabs of ice from our bow with his long harpoon. We landed at a small beach where the gentle wave action had cleared the snow leaving a long strip of rounded pebbles and larger rocks. In front of us was a long white slope of fresh snow leading up to the rocky headland above. There were indeed penguins on this shore and some had settled on a small rocky promontory to our right. What a fascinating sight we beheld! From the rocky promontory, two distinct and deep tracks ran up the snow slope to the penguin rookery perched high up on the protected side of the headland. This was my first close encounter with these amiable little birds for they were what I later found in the journals of my library to be Gentoo Penguins.

As both boats were now up on the stony beach, we watched with some curiosity and wonder at the social organisation of these little birds. They were about two feet tall and stood very erect. Their white breast and back backs and small heads with a white cap and with long, narrow wings reminded me somewhat of a small butler ready to serve his master with some treat or other. They waddled along with their wings out-stretched to keep their balance, much like a child walking along a narrow gutter in such a quaint manner that some of the men pointed to them and laughed. The nature of the two deep tracks running up through the snow slope soon became apparent. One track was reserved for dirty penguins coming down from their high rookery heading for the sea and the other was for the clean penguins coming back from their fishing excursions taking their swallowed catch back to their nests. There were a few tracks down closer to the beach which ran along parallel to the shore. The little Gentoos often waddled along, walking in line one after the other in small groups.

"Like a line of drunken sailormen just a'comin from the inn!" scoffed Mr Warren with a laugh. For they did remind us all of an ordered line of sailors moving purposely along their track with a shambling gait. Occasionally one penguin, either confused about its course towards its rookery or simply rebelling against tradition – there are those in all societies – would venture up the downward track. Doing this it would soon encounter a line of dirty penguins coming down from above. There would be a slight touching of beaks and a general inspection before the wayward penguin would be forced to step aside and allow his betters to continue their journey to the sea. Everything was done in such a formal manner that my comparison to a gentleman's gentleman seemed to be in order.

Not wishing to follow suit and disturb these delightful little birds, we cut our own track up through the snow at some distance to those of the penguins. Ours was a new track and we found that the snow was deeper than we had imagined. It was also wider and as we climbed, we noticed that a few of these little birds, who had no fear of humans whatsoever,

The penguin roads

The rookery

followed us up our track. Some type of penguin highway, they undoubtedly thought!

Reaching the rookery, we found that the noise of their shrill cries and the smell was quite disturbing. Their nests were of small round hollows made by carefully dropping small stones around in a circle. We had noticed that a few of the birds coming up our trail carried pebbles from the beach below, but they were more often inclined to steal stones from a neighbour's nest. This of course, resulted in a loud squabble which accounted for much of the noise in the rookery. The smell from their guano, which covered much of the area around the nests, was a pungent combination of rotten fish and wet poultry. It was very unpleasant but the effects were soon lost in the fascination of watching these birds at their social activities of the rookery, guarding their nests and coming from and going to the sea.

Many of the men who had spent most of their adult life in Arctic waters had not seen penguins in their native state before as these birds only inhabit the Southern Hemisphere from the cold waters of the Antarctic to almost tropical waters near the Galapagos Islands well to the north. Some of the men were intent on killing some of these birds to supplement the fish and whale which were now their only source of fresh meat. It was known to some of the experienced hands who had served in the southern oceans that penguin meat was an acceptable fare, tasting somewhat like a combination of beef and cod and also was reputed in being able to prevent scurvy. Having watched these amiable little creatures waddling back and forth going about their industrious lives, and having a well-stocked larder onboard the *Australis*, we decided to take a few eggs and leave their owners alone.

We were not the only predators of these lovely little birds for nearby on a high rock stood a waiting Skua. They are medium-sized seabird with a generally brown to grey plumage with white tips on their outer wings. They have a wingspan of over four feet and their beak ends in a vicious hook. They like penguin chicks and eggs and I am told that most penguin rookeries have at least one resident Skua. This particular bird had taken exception to our incursion into its territorial claims and later skimmed low over our boat with a raucous cry.

Even at sea where they are very fast swimmers, penguins are subject to predation. Only the day previously we had passed a large floe at some distance upon which stood three lonely Chinstrap penguins[7]. They stood perfectly still, like a line of toy soldiers in their black and white uniforms standing to attention. The crew wondered why they stood so still during the several minutes in which we passed the flow. Suddenly the reason for their motionless behaviour became apparent as the large dorsal fins of two Orcas[8]

---

[7] The Chinstrap penguin (*Pygoscelis antarcticus*) name derives from the narrow black band under its head which makes it appear as if it were wearing a black helmet. They stand about 70 cm. high..

[8] The Orca (*Orcinus Orca*) or 'killer whale' is a toothed whale which often hunts in packs for penguins, seals and other marine mammals. They have been known to rapidly circle an ice flow containing penguins or seals so as to overturn it to get to the animals.

broke the surface just near the edge of the flow. A third fin broke the surface just behind the other two.

My musing over the apparent abundance of life and its' savagery in this bleak land which is unhospitable to mankind was suddenly broken by an unexpected cry from one of our men who had climbed up higher on the rocky headland.

"Ship, ho! Well off in yonder bay." He cried, pointing away to the south.
I climbed up to him and followed his outstretched arm which pointed into the next bay.

"Lookee thar, cap'n," he said, still pointing into the wide bay that was cut well into the steep, rocky sides of the island south of our headland. I took out my small, portable telescope which I had carried in my coat to sight in the direction of his gaze.

Sure enough, there was a ship hard up against the further shore of the bay. I focussed the lens for a clearer view and saw that it was barque-rigged and looking well worse for wear. It was a wreck of a whaler, there was no doubt with part of its bow submerged and two of its masts down and draped across its deck.

Climbing down from our rocky lookout as fast as I could manage, not being a good climber, I quickly called:

"Mr Warren, lively now. There's a wreck up yonder bay which needs some inspection. We will take Krystof, Lars, Taumalolo and some of the older hands in my boat and the others can stay with the second boat to get the ice. Have one of the older hands report to Mr. Turling when they get back to tell him what we are about and to have the ship ready to sail should we need him."

All of us half ran and half slipped down the snowy slope to our boats below. Lars, being from the snow-covered mountains of Sweden lay on his back and slid down the snow like some crazy sled with arms and legs flying.

It was an easy row around the point but still it took some time as the wreck was probably about two or three miles from the *Australis*. The oars dipped in regular strokes and our crews put their backs into it, such was their eagerness to get to the wreck. On our way around the rocky point we came under a cliff face which contained a long, sheltered guano-covered ledge upon which a number of black cormorants clustered in their rocky nests. Soon we were out in ice-strewn water and coming nearer to the hulk.

"Up oars!" I cried as we rounded a small flow and glided in the still water up to the weather-beaten wooden hull.

"She's a whaler, alright!" exclaimed Caleb Warren.

As our boat touched the old hulk, Lars jumped to the main chains which held the standing rigging to the hull. With a cry he fell back into the boat.

"Å, tømmeret er råttent!" he exclaimed in his native Norwegian[9] forgeting his years on a Yankee ship and holding a piece of the gun'le which had given way to his grasp.

"Steady, now!" I cried to the other boat. "She may be a little frail after all of these years."

Lars once again climbed onto the main chains but was careful to test his handhold until he felt secure.

"Ya! She's full uf vater, alright!" he exclaimed. "No deck, yair!"

Without a firm deck to walk upon, we polled our way around to the large stern windows.
"Em's bin sip nem belong 'Cetacean', Cap'n Boss" said Taumalolo. "Em bilong 'Tucket longtime pass"[10], he continued.

"She's the *Cetacean* from Nantucket." I spoke to Caleb Warren who sat in the stern sheets of our boat.

---

[9] "Oh, the timber is rotten!"

[10] Pidgin English – a composite language system used by many Pacific Islanders and here meaning "Its' name is the 'Cetacean', Captain, from Nantucket a long time ago."

"Aye," replied the first mate. "She's from Nantucket, all right. Cap'n Cornelius Coffey was her captain back in '42. Not much left now, I'm a thinking."

"No, Mr Warren. Not much left". I replied as I used an oar to push open one of the stern windows. The great cabin, for she was an old design which still retained a single large stern cabin, was also full of water. The faint light of the fading Antarctic day rippled across the cross-members of the cabin's dark ceiling. The ship was cold and lifeless and had been for many years.

"Well, whatever cause took her this so far south to her icy grave will stay with her," I said with some reverence for the men who had manned her. "Her stern davit is empty, you see, so perhaps some men escaped but it's unlikely that they made it out of this wilderness."

"Sir, there's something dark a'sticken out of the snow over there on the shore!" cried Seth Rowlings, one of our old hands who was at the lead oar.

I followed his outstretched arm and focussed my small telescope on the small, dark shape standing out in the white snow. It was the bow of a ship's boat half embedded in the ice on the opposite shore.

Rowling's eyes were very good for such an old hand for the shore was a good row away. I motioned for Caleb Warren turn our boat and steer in that direction.

"Wanpela samting kam hariap![11]" cried Taumalolo, standing up in the bow and pointing to the open water out in the bay. He had taken up his harpoon which he always carried and now braced himself for a throw.

The narrow bay was now a mix of small ice floes separated by patches of open water. At about fifty yards, the small floes were being pushed away by a small arrowhead of a wave which streamed back on either side of whatever was under the water and moving rapidly towards us.

"Wait!" I cried, standing up in the boat and taking hold Taumalolo's arm. The wave had disappeared and the water was again still. Suddenly a long, dark shape glided alongside the boat. It was a small whale; a Minke whale[12] just slightly longer than our boat. As it glided past, it rolled over so that its large eye gazed up at us. It surfaced briefly just past our stern, its dorsal fin breaking the grey water and pushing away several small ice floes.

"Thar's anuther!" cried Seth Rowlings and several of the men had stood up in the boat to follow his out-stretched arm.

Indeed, there were two Minke whales, probably a mating couple, who had been curious about these new interlopers

---

[11] Pidgin English – "Somethings coming quickly!"

[12] Antarctic Minke whale or southern Minke whale (*Balaenoptera bonaerensis*), is a small baleen whale with a grey-black body about 7 metres long and feeds on small marine crustaceans or krill.

which floated upon their sea. These were undoubtedly the Antarctic or southern strain of their species. They were of a dark grey colour and were baleen whales. That is, they fed on minute sea creatures by straining them through strips of baleen; a forest of bristles in their upper mouth which acts like a filter to obtain their food. They were no threat to us unless they were panicked and accidently upset our boat.

"Sit down!" I ordered. "They are only curious Minkes and mean us no harm."

The two whales circled our boat for a short time and then together they arched their backs and dived deeper below the surface never to be seen again.

We had quite forgotten our task for a moment but now the men took up their oars and we continued our journey to the opposite shore. In a short while we were opposite a small ice ledge at the base of a steep slope of ice and new snow. Out of this, the fragile timbers of an old whaling boat projected. Some of the faded white paint still remained on the rotten hull planks – for she was clinker-built[13] like most of our small boats.

Pulling alongside the ice shelf, the men jumped ashore and secured our anchor into the ice. We examined the interior of the boat which had her stern embedded in the white wall but otherwise seemed to be empty. None of the usual

---

[13] Clinker-built: boats made of long planks which are overlapped around the hull.

paraphernalia found in the bow of a whaling skiff was to be seen but the men had found something near the stern of the boat which was partly embedded in the ice. It was a small barrel.

Using his trusty harpoon, Taumalolo chipped away at the ice until one of the men was able to pull the barrel clear. He suddenly dropped it with a coarse oath.

"Gud almighty! It's gunpowder!" He exclaimed.

Sure enough, it was a small wooden keg of gunpowder, a little over a foot across. Some of the other men laughed at their companion's fright. There were in fact five small barrels.

"Not to worry, matey" laughed Rowlings. "It'll take more then you're rough handlin' to set er orf, I'm thinkin!".

Mr Warren came up to my side and said in a low voice." Cap'n Jamie, the sea is takin' on that greasy look. I fear it is all going to turn to ice soon and we are a long way from the ship."

"Aye, you're not wrong in that, Caleb. See how some of the thin plates of ice have already formed and are being quickly broken into many small leads." I turned to the small group of men who were still looking over the old whaler. "It's time we headed back. Into the boats, men!" I cried, picking up the small keg of gunpowder from the bottom of the old

The whaleboat frozen in the ice

And the sea began to freeze

whaler. "This may come in handy for our Fourth of July celebrations." I joked.

Our way back to the *Australis* was now blocked by a jigsaw pattern of many small ice floes separated by small patches of open water, the surface of which had taken on a greasy due to the formation of a thin layer of ice. Seawater freezes at about twenty-eight degrees Fahrenheit[14] and the slight currents in the water break up the newly-formed ice sheets giving the surface a cracked-like appearance.

It was difficult for the men to row because of their oars slipping on the ice as we passed each flow. Taumalolo stood in the bow of the boat and attempted to push the smaller floes out of our path. All the while he quietly sung a dirge-like song in his native tongue; a sign that he was extremely worried and feared death. A large leopard seal watched with some indifference from a nearby flow.
Eventually we came to within hailing distance of our ship and I stood up and, cupping my hands to my mouth called out:

"Mr Turling! All the hands to get ready to make sail…belay that! Have Mr Dunsmuir get up steam." My change in orders came about due to the realisation that our most obvious course would be south around the big island; right into the wind which had now freshened and snow was

---

[14] This is about -2 degrees Celsius and the lower temperature is due to the salt content.

beginning to fall. It would take all of our brave little engine's power to push through this jigsaw of ice and snow.

Chapter Nine
Trapped in the Ice
Latitude 64°12' 55" South; Longitude 62° 46' 31" West
-5⁰F, high winds 40 knots from the South

All out boats secured and the engine throbbing away we headed the *Australis* south and then west around the southerly tip of the big island. The men seemed to be of better cheer as our new course meant that we were headed into warmer climes.

Our joy unfortunately was short lived, for later that day we rounded the southwestern tip of the island for whilst the wind still continued to blow from the south, it had greatly strengthened and despite it not yet being winter, the temperature had dropped alarmingly as the cold air descended upon the sea straight from the pole. Moreover, we had thought to find an open sea now that we had quitted the confines of the straits between the mainland and its off-shore islands. But no! In front of us was a vast expanse of white; a jumbled jigsaw pattern of ice floes covered in a light dusting of snow. There was little clear water between them and even there the surface had that greasy appearance of water in the act of turning to ice.

However, our gallant *Australis* had been built to face such obstacles and she ploughed ahead at a good four knots. Where she could not push the floes aside, she rose up and slid upon them so that her ice-strengthened bow would crush the ice by the her very weight. Mr Dunsmuir came up on deck to see how his engine was taking our ship through the ice field.

"Well noo! is nae thon a great sicht! we coud no dae thon under sail!" he proudly boasted. A smile of satisfaction on his broad, whiskered face.

"Aye, indeed Mr. Dunsmuir," replied Caleb Warren, "our stout ship is doing very well, thank'ee."

Despite the wind and the cold, we were greatly cheered by our ship's progress through the broken ice field and the men seemed to feel this also as they went about their duties on deck. We had taken down all sail at our previous anchorage and now bumped our way through the ice, a thick cloud of smoke and steam coming from our tall smokestack blowing out over our bow. In the foc'sle a cheering song could be heard coming as the men off duty were pleased that we were heading north.

It was the second day of our progress close into the big island which we had rounded, when our happiness and the motion of the *Australis* suddenly stopped. It was in the first part of the evening watch when a sudden loud noise came from the stern accompanied by a severe shudder which went through the entire ship. I rushed to the aft steering house and grabbed the brass speaking tube which led down into the engine room.

"Stop the engine!" I shouted.

"Och aye! A think thon has already happenit. It sounds as gin we have hit something, Captain." Mr Dunsmuir's laconic voice came up through the tube. "A'll come up an be wi ye directly".

By now many of the crew had gathered around the aft deck house to see what had happed. Mr Dunsmuir had come up from the engine room and he, Caleb Warren, and I were now at the stern railing looking down at the icy blue water below. There was still a clear, jagged pathway of clear water stretching out from our stern into the vast whiteness of the icefield beyond.

"A canna see anything!" exclaimed our engineer.

"No, the problem must lie deep below," responded the first mate.

I turned to the assembled crew standing on and around the deck house and gave an order to our second mate.

"Mr Turling! Take all the hands you can muster and move all of our cargo and ballast towards the bow. We need to raise the stern as far as possible."

"Aye, sir," came a distant reply from the rear of the crowd followed by a few words of command as the crew disappeared to carry out my order. My two companions and I returned to the railing and optimistically searched the clear waters for the cause of our troubles.

It took several hours of hard work below decks before the stern with its long rudder shaft and propeller railing began to emerge from the water. By now, the ice had all but closed in and filled the spaces past our stern.

Any attempt at hauling up the propeller using the chains which were shackled to the sides of the hinged propeller shaft proved fruitless. Under normal conditions, when the ship's propulsion changed from steam to sail, the propeller would be hauled up its guiding rails so that it would remain locked out of the water so as not to impede the motion of the ship. Now there was no movement.

"Och! dae ye see thare? ane o the blades seems a mite twistit," said our engineer pointing down to the vague shape of our bronze propeller which could only just been seen below the water.

"Aye, Mr Dunsmuir," said Caleb Warren, "it looks like we have hit something indeed."

"More likely a large fragment of ice pushed below by our ice-breaking," I ventured, "can we do anything about it, Mr Dunsmuir?"
"Och, aye, but no here. It wad tak a brave man tae gae under thae waters tae free our prop," he replied. "He wouldnae last twa minutes i thon icy water!"

"Right then!" I replied, "Let us make as much sail as we can and try to make headway."

"All hands to make sail!" cried Mr Warren, rushing down the side of the deck cabin.

With the wind blowing strongly from our stern, we dared only to run before it under reduced sail lest we had our masts carried away.

With our sails stretched to their limit and the ship now restored to its normal stability, we made little headway through the icefield. Eventually our motion slowed as the ice piled up against our bow. There was not enough momentum to lift it up and over the larger floes to break through them. The ship was now trapped within the ice.

The hopelessness of the situation fell upon us like the grey cover of clouds above. There was no sunshine here and even the horizon had become a vague unbroken line of white against the grey of the clouds. The big island which was off our starboard beam was no longer visible, only the sea of white snow and a faint track where are ship had been.

"Have the men furl all the sails and then come to the foc'sle." I asked Mr Warren and went into the Chart Room which was at the rear of the aft deckhouse. Here I hoped to get some perspective as to what I should do next. There seemed no way forward yet I had to be able to reassure the crew that all was not lost. Here was nothing but a short respite from the cold wind which blew hard over our stern and mocked our lack of motion through the sea of ice. What could we do now but try to make the best of our frozen anchorage and wait until the sea again opened up and released us? Above me I heard the shriek of the wind through our standing rigging and the faint call of Mr Turling calling orders through his speaking trumpet to the topmen aloft.

After a time, which seemed an eternity, I buttoned up my sea coat and walked along the deck towards the foc'sle forward. A light fall of snow had begun to cover the deck with a soft, crystal whiteness which hid its malice in its beauty.

I knocked on the door of the foc'sle as was the custom, for the captain of a ship was not free to enter the crew's domain without their permission. Caleb Warren opened the door and bade me enter. It was warm and comfortable here. The central pot-bellied stove and the domestic nature of the men's slung hammocks and personal belongings would normally make this a place of cheer. Now the men sat at the table or stood around the stove with looks of apprehension upon their honest, weather-beaten faces. I moved into the centre of the room and looked around. I was their captain but most of the men were old enough to be my father. Indeed, many of them had sailed with father on his ships in the waters of the North Atlantic for many a year. Now I was but a young man with the burden of command upon my shoulders. What could I tell them about the sea and the ice which they knew so well?

"Well, we have been stopped," I said in light-hearted tone which belied the desperate situation in which we were in.

"Do not be too alarmed," I lied as I was not convinced in myself where fate would now take us. I hid my feeling of despair and continued.
"It looks bad at the moment, but I am confident that this is but a short disruption to our journey north. The wind outside has brought an unexpected chill not typical of the season and when it drops, we will find free water again. Our propeller has jammed but we are in good sailing order and will fly again soon when we have good sea room."

"Aye, well enough, captain," spoke Seth Rowlings from his hammock nearby. He was one of the most experienced seamen in the crew and had sailed the Cape Horn route many a time, "but wha' about this ice? We are trapped here now and if this weather doesnay stop then we a be locked in like the old *Aquinnah* whose bones lie below the Arctic ice!"

There was a low murmur about the room for many of the men had been with my father on that ill-fated cruise when his ship was crushed in the ice in the Greenland Sea. Men had died, most had suffered, and now were we to meet the same fate?

"Listen men!" I exclaimed. This is not the *Aquinnah* but the *Australis*. It was designed and built by men who knew that we would probably meet the ice; my father and that renowned shipwright Peder Andersen who has never lost a ship! It is built to withstand such a fate. Ice cannot crush this ship! Its hull is shaped and strengthened to rise up above the power of the crush. All we have to do is wait until the weather calms and the temperature rises and then the sea will again be open to us."

There was no response from the men who looked down and about the warm foc'sle. Perhaps this may have been partly shame in doubting my promises, or the reputation of my father or perhaps the trust in a ship-builder like Andersen. Whatever their feelings, no man answered and no eye met mine. Caleb Warren, the true seaman and friend that he was pushed forward and spoke.

"Now, men. Ye' heard the Captain. We have no fear of the ice in this ship! She's well founded and built for jest this type of sea." He turned to the second mate, "Mr Turling, have the duty watch break out those new-fangled steam hoses and let's get some of this ice off'n our decks. The rest of you I want to secure tha ship. Lash all the loose gear and make sure all of the sheets and rigging are tight! Right! Get on with it!"

There was a short confusion of men as the duty watch and many of the others left the foc'sle.

"Thank'ee, Mr Warren," I said as I followed the last man out. He gave me the faintest smile on his grim face but I knew that he was as worried about the situation as I. He was a good leader of men and knew that they would be worried less if they went about the tasks at hand. He and Turling climbed up onto the raised bow to supervise the men now securing the ship whilst I walked aft to my cabin.

The length of daylight had become suddenly short at this latitude and there were only a few hours difference between sunrise a few hours before noon and sunset a few hours later. It was not yet the end of the afternoon watch yet darkness was creeping over the ship like a shroud. In my cabin I lay on my bunk in a deep fit of melancholy. Thoughts came and went into my head like a parade of phantoms come to torment my sanity. Had I misled the men? Our ship was certainly designed to withstand the worst of the sea ice in the north, but would the southern ice pack be more severe in its treatment of our vessel? Would the weather continue in this severe cold blast so early in the season? Did this wind bode ill for us all and we would be marooned here in this vast expanse of white for ever? These were the dreadful thoughts which plague my mind as I fell into a fitful slumber.

I awoke with a sudden shock of incomprehension. I was still fully dressed and it was dark and cold in the cabin; the oil in the lamb on the wall in its polished gimbal had been exhausted and the coals in the small stove had turned to grey ash. I grabbed my sea-coat and scarf and quickly felt my way up on deck. It was dark still and very cold. The harsh southerly wind still blew as strong as ever and the cabin roof cleared from snow a few hours before was again covered in a thick layer of white. There was a small lantern at the aft steering station where a lone seaman stood watch. He was heavily dressed in his coat and woollen cap even with the comfort of the small heating pipes near the wheel. Mr Dunsmuir had kept steam up in the engine room and we would at least be warm below decks as well as here.

"Mornin,' Cap'n" he said, knuckling his forehead. It was young Sanders, one of Mr Turling's watch who stood by the helm. It seemed foolish for a man to be at the wheel when the ship was motionless and had nowhere to go. But at least he was sheltered from the wind and was as warm as one could be on deck.

"Good morning, Sanders." I replied. "No drop in the wind, I see?"

"Ah, no sir. It's been'a blowing like this all night she was. An' the snow's bin a fallin'."

I went back into the chartroom and gathered up some of the old charts and sea logs which may have some knowledge of our position and the kind of conditions which usually beset these regions. Soon I heard voices as the watch changed and new men took their stations. With no chance of collision at sea, we had reduced the watch to just two men; one at the helm and another poor soul in the shelter of the foc'sle entrance. Gradually there were other muffled sounds below deck where the shrieking sounds of the wind was muffled by the deck and its covering of snow. My officers were awake and no doubt the cook, Jacob Simmonds was stoking up the large stove in his galley below ready for the morning meal. Life on board went on.

There was little to do on a stationary ship in the middle of an icefield with a howling strong and bitter wind. The men for the most part stayed in their snug foc'sle around their coal stove and tried to keep busy. Some went about the mundane task of mending their clothes whilst others took on more artistic diversions, such as the carving of whalebone of which we had plenty in store. This is called scrimshaw and it has been a sailor's craft in whaling vessels for many a year. The schrimshanders, for so these men referred to themselves, would take some of the best shapes of whalebone, clean and polish it and then carve it into interesting shapes, upon this many intricate designs were then scratched. Often it included an outline of their ship or of a loved one ashore with some endearing turn of phrase about life and loneliness upon the sea. In the northern waters of the Arctic, walrus tusks were most favoured and sometimes the teeth of the sperm whale. Other men used some of the scraps from Lar's wood store to make ship models and others platted rope into sandals, baskets and mats.

Whilst we retained our traditional watch system, there was little to watch out for but occasionally the watch and even all hands would be called out to perform some important duty. The men thus called would come up on deck with a sullen indifference. It was usually dark and very cold and all the while the wind howled its defiance through our rigging.

By the third day in the ice, the pressure of the ice pushing in from all sides caused our ship to rise up slightly and tilt at a few degrees. There had been a significant amount of snow piling up on the deck and also aloft. Our yards now hung with so many small icicles that I feared that this additional weight might cause the yardarms or even the upper masts to collapse. Accordingly, I ordered all hands up on deck for removing the weight of snow and ice which now covered our ship daily. Our efforts were greatly helped by our steam hoses; a provision of our visionary shipwright, Peder Andersen. When rigged, we were able to play a jet of stream some distance across the deck as Mr Dunsmuir had ensured that our boilers were full pressure. This was done with extreme caution as a high-powered jet of steam would be fatal for any man who stepped in its path. So, it was done using one team of three men, two to hold and direct the hose and the other as lookout to ensure that the jet was directed where it should be. Once our yards were clear of ice, the steam hoses would be shut off and the topmen would clamber up and across the yards to furl the canvas into a tighter, more secure bundles along the upper surfaces of the yards. In more permanent anchorages the sails would be completely removed from the yards, but my

Trapped in the ice

officers and I felt that such an act would suggest such a permanent stay in the ice so we decided to leave the canvas on our yards readying for sailing when our luck changed. It was however, a more routine action to lower the upper yards and reduce the weight upon the upper masts and thus prevent our ship from becoming top heavy. This being done, the men again retreated to the comfort of their quarters. It now only required a small team of men to emerge each day during our few hours of daylight to again remove any build-up of ice on the yards and deck. Below decks our cook, Jacob Simmons, in his perpetually warm galley, grumbled about his job as usual but more so as Mr Warren had ordered him to be less generous with our supplies. In this respect we were in good order; we had been well supplied and as the *Australis* was designed for long-distance cruising, we had plenty of storage space for our bountiful supply of provisions. Moreover, the crew had often taken advantage of some of their spare time to catch fish and the occasional unwary seal. There was even a goodly supply of penguin eggs taken from a rookery on Deception Island.

At dinner that night in the officers' dining cabin we discussed our options and possibilities for the future. Whilst I had enormous faith in the strength of our ship to survive the ice, this sentiment was not shared by the others. Caleb Warren had sailed with father for a long time and trusted in his judgement and therefore shared some of my faith in our ship's worth, but the others had been too long in frail, wooden ships in the Arctic to accept my reassurances.

Mr Turling in particular was most pessimistic in his comments. He was a good second mate but tended to be limited in his patience with the crew and any situation which would place considerable stress upon his shoulders. "With all due respects to you and the designers of this ship Captain, I cannot see much hope in waiting for the weather to clear and free us from the ice. We should strike out with the boats and look for open water," he exclaimed forcefully.

"Och aye. We ha' plenty o coal for steam but we canna run the engine until we free tha propeller. Anywa' we are heald here an' nowhere tae gae!" said our engineer who was at quite a loss now that his beloved engine was useless.

"Well, now!" said Caleb Warren, taking his pipe from his mouth and tapping the cold ashes into the tray at his elbow." It appears ta me that we have little choice. We are surrounded by ice and snow and even during the day the cloud is just above us and we are lucky to see one side o the ship from t'other."

"We must have faith in the strength of the *Australis* and that this unseasonal wind and cold will soon die down. Then you'll see the ice break up and we can do the best we can to free her and get to open water," I replied with as much false optimism which I could muster, for at present I could not see any change in our unhappy condition. We dined in silence and then retired to our cabins without the usual good-natured conversation and cigar which we usually had after our evening meal.

Ships are never quiet places of abode. Even at the dock in some quiet port there is always the gentle lap of water upon the hull, the sounds of soft creaking of timbers and rigging and the careful tread of the night anchor watch making his lonely rounds checking the security of the ship.

Tonight, it was the unusual sounds which disturbed my rest; the frightful sudden groan of timbers as the ice pressed in from all sides and the distant sound of the winds howling through the rigging. Caleb Warren had joked at the table tonight about poor O'Leary the Irish stoker[1] who swore to all of his shipmates that the wind was the cry of some Celtic banshee come to herald our doom.

I was a hard-headed Yankee and did not believe in such stuff and nonsense but still the incessant noise of the wind and the sound of the pack ice upon the ship ensured that it was a fitful night.

I was suddenly awoken out of my nightmares of ice and of my father and his men of the *Aquinnah* perishing on the frozen lands at the opposite end of the Earth. There, now in the darkness and chill of my cabin there was a long, low

---

[1] A crew member of the engine room who stoked the boilers with coal. An expression still used for some of the modern engine room staff.

grinding sound and the feeling that my bunk was being tilted over by some rogue wave.

The ice had moved suddenly and pushed the *Australis* over to an alarming angle.

Chapter Ten
Abandon Ship!
Position unknown
3⁰F, high winds 35 knots from the South

The ship had tilted over to port in a most alarming manner. I stumbled about the dark cabin, disorientated by the angle of the deck. Finding my boots and my heavy sea coat, I managed to open the door and go out on deck. There was a light where the foc'sle door had opened and the men were now also coming out on deck in a state of bewilderment and fear. Some slipped on the icy deck and slid down to the gun'le.

Mr Turling, the second mate was already in their midst shouting for every man to return to his hammock. I went aft, going hand-over-hand along the icy starboard railing. Caleb Warren came out of his cabin, hanging onto the door which swung closed as soon as he reached the railing.

"This doesn't look good, Jamie!" he said, the urgency being underscored by the familiar use of my Christian name.

"No, Caleb." I answered. "Get Lars to take some men and sound the hull below decks. We need to know whether this sudden crush has sprung the timbers."

I reached the foc'sle to find total chaos. The men were sitting at the table of lying in their hammocks all talking at once. Mr Turling's voice was raised to quell the confusion but without much success other than to add to the cacophony. The noise slowly dropped as I entered.

"Hold on, men!" I shouted. "Our ship is not lost yet! Lars the carpenter is now inspecting our hull and I am sure that he will find it sound. This is just a small aberration of the ice. You'll soon see. We will once more get to an even keel."

There were a few ominous growls from the rear of the foc'sle and old Seth Rawlings spoke up in his strong voice:

"Aye, perhaps so, Cap'n. But it doesn't look so good now. It was like this in the early times o' the poor *Aquinnah* afore she broke up. We should look to our own safety ashore on the ice."

"Very well, I replied. At first light we will start to unload all that we need on the ice. I'll have Ezekiel Chapman make up some tents from our spare sailcloth and we will live off the ship in case she breaks up. Is that what you men want?" I asked.

There were mutterings of 'aye's' from around the crowded foc'sle and the door opened behind me. It was Lars the carpenter.

"Der ship es most sund, Capitan. Ver lit vater." He said softly, a smile of relief on his broad face.

"Thank you, Lars," I said. "there you see, men. The ship is sound and so we have little chance of sinking, however we will follow through and set up our tents at first light. In the meantime, get your own personal kits ready in case we decide to live on the ice. I'll have Mr Dunsmuir the engineer see if his men cannot make some small stoves for your comfort." With this I turned, giving Caleb Warren a concerned look as we walked back to my cabin.

"Well, Captain," he said formally. "We are listing about twenty degrees to port according to the inclinometer in the wheelhouse. I doubt that we have the manpower to restore trim on her."

"No, Mr Warren." I replied. "It looks like we are going to be askew for a while. Take what volunteers you can get and lower the aft topmast, as it looks like it will topple soon."

Whilst Caleb Warren and his men climbed the rigging to remove the aft topmast, that highest part of our rear mast, the men in the foc'sle were busy collecting their own belongings and lashing up their hammocks ready to go to their new quarters. At the first glimmer of faint light through the low cloud, they began moving stores and other equipment down onto the ice. Mr Turling had ordered that the port cutting stage be lowered to act as a ramp down which the men could lower some of the heavier supplies. They had spread rubber deck mats down this make-shift ramp; the same mats we often used when cutting up the whales on deck so as to stop our feet slipping in the blood.

Our new 'village' of tents was set up about a hundred yards from the ship; there now being a perimeter of broken slabs of pack ice pushed up around its hull in a series of pressure ridges where the ice floes had collided and rode up upon each other.

Some of the men, under Seth Rawling's instruction were using saws and shovels to cut large blocks of ice from a flow at some distance from the camp. These were being used as windbreaks around the tents as the southerly wind still blew hard across the icy waste.

Whether it was a matter of expediency or some old hang-up from some older traditions, but my officers and I decided to stay in our tilted cabins onboard the *Australis*. Lars the carpenter, Ezekiel Chapman the sailmaker and Jacob Simmons our cook also elected to stay onboard for their berths were still snug in their own little worlds. Mr Dunsmuir, of course stayed in his cabin so that he could keep an eye on his beloved boiler and engine. His three stokers also had no intension of moving from their warm billets near the engine room and had rigged hammocks in the companionway nearby. Luckily, our new orientation had little effect on the engine room and boiler save that the door to the boiler had to be propped open when it was being stoked with coal. This being done, our boiler was kept at only a minimal pressure. A similar situation also occurred in the galley. Our large stove which was needed for cooking and source of hot water also had its doors mounted athwart[1] the ship. Whilst this meant that some extra effort was required to open the heavy oven door, it also meant that the firebox could still be primed with fuel. Unfortunately, the poor trim of the oven also meant that the boilers into which the men's ration of salt junk[2] was cooked could only be filled halfway making the cooking process more time-consuming.

So, our poor *Australis* became partly deserted. Some of us stayed onboard and tried to make ourselves busy with minor tasks; I read and re-read the old whaling journals, especially the maps of Nathaniel Palmer hoping to find some inspiration for the future, Mr Dunsmuir and his stokers went about their usual tasks in the engine room maintaining some steam pressure and Mr Turling and Caleb Warren did their best to encourage the crew to find their own ways of getting through the short, gloomy day and long brooding darkness of night. General maintenance of the poor *Australis'* decks and upper works were gradually reduced to nothing as a deep malaise set in. Snow, then ice built up upon the rooves of the deckhouses and on the board central deck. We had become an ice ship in an ice sea.

It was now into the third week of the period of strong southerly wind, bitterly cold weather and reduced visibility. Sitting in the cold chartroom, I was again going

---

[1] Across the axis of the ship i.e. from side to side so that the oven door faced forward rather than to one side.

[2] Salted meat

over the old chart of Palmer when I heard a joyous cry from the deck above. One of the more optimistic sailors, indeed it was the irrepressible Krystof, was yelling something in his heavily-accented English. He had climbed up to the first top of the foremast in a vain attempt to look for a clear horizon. I later learned from Mr Warren that in the last week this was a regular undertaking by this enthusiastic man.

Going out on deck I could now clearly hear his cries for the wind had dropped now to a mere stiff breeze.

"Land! I hav' seeing tha' land. Offa thar to starboard!"

I ran forward, slipping on the occasional patch of ice where the snow drifts had been worn down and climbed the ratlines to join Krystof at the first top of the foremast. He had borrowed one of the ship's telescopes from Mr Turling and had been looking at anything which made a solid appearance in the gloom of the low cloud and fog. He handed the glass to me and gestured over our port beam. Sure enough, there was a vague demarcation between the intense flat surface of our ice see and a darker line where the ice met land. Many of the crew had climbed up onto the ship and now looked earnestly in the direction which Krystof was now pointing and waving his arms in excitement. Visible land! Perhaps our luck was changing and I felt that there was yet hope for our poor ship.

Over the span of the short day, the cloud did indeed lift. It was still low and foreboding but now a distinct horizon could be seen around all quarters of the ship. The men had clambered into the rigging or stood upon the heaped snowdrifts of the foc'sle and deck house and jumped and danced with glee. The wind also was dropping and I hoped that this would herald the return of warmer weather and the release of the ship.

My hope was dashed later in the day when I saw teams of men hammering away at some of our whalers which they had taken down from the deck and onto the ice. Caleb Warren came to me with a dark look upon his face and his cap in his hand.

"Cap'n Jaimie," he said in a low voice. "I'm sorry, but the men want to quit the *Australis*."

"Why?" I looked up from my desk rather bewildered at this sudden turn of events.

My first mate and old friend looked away for a second then turned and faced me directly.

"They have seen some cracks in the surface of the ice and from the foretop think that there is possibly a deep lead[3] off our bow before the horizon. They want to leave the ship

---

[3] Leads are narrow, linear cracks in the ice that form when ice floes diverge. These may open out and connect to the sea.

and strike in that direction man-hauling the whalers to the open sea and then sailing north. They are not deserting, Cap'n Jaimie for they want all of us to go, including you."

"But this is senseless now with the weather clearing. The very cracks that they have seen means that we will soon be restored to our usual trim and may even be able to break free if such a lead comes to the ship," I replied.

Leaving the cabin, I went down to the group of men who were now busily nailing tight canvas across the bows of the whalers as protection against wind and sea. Mr Turling was in their midst and I approached him directly.

"What is going on here, Mr Turling?" I asked.

"Why sir, we thought it best to get the whalers ready for sea. There's an opening in the ice yonder and a chance to escape this accursed land. I thought that it would be an expedient thing to do."

"Aye, perhaps." I replied, not wishing to countermand the order of this officer, "but it may be yet premature to think that the *Australis* is going to stay locked here forever. We had better call the men together in the foc'sle and hear their feelings."

I turned and walked back to my cabin, leaving my two senior officers to gather up the crew and send them to the foc'sle. I had not anticipated this action from the men but it was probably understandable. Many of them had survived one entrapment in the Arctic ice and now the situation looked similar, even with a slight change in the weather.

Now in the foc'sle and with the entire crew sitting or standing before me I again reiterated the special ice-proof nature of the ship and an optimistic future. But to no avail. Various crewmen spoke up; some with experience of the ice and others out of fear. The general feeling was one of optimism if the ship was deserted. Mr Turling who supported the idea outlined the plan.

The whalers could be re-fitted to take extra men. They had their usual mast and set of sails and with some weather-proofing in the form of canvas over the open hulls between mast and bow, there would be some protection from the waves and wind. Moreover, each boat would have one of the small stoves made by Mr Dunsmuir's men and a good supply of coal and provisions of which we had a plenty. The plan required me to lead the group across the ice as my father had done from the stricken *Aquinnah* those many year ago. Once we had reached the deep lead we would row or raise the sail and head north in groups of three of two boats each tethered together. Their aim was to strike out north and east to find the islands which parallel the mainland. With luck, we could again reach Deception Island and rest in the warmth of the hot springs before heading on the long journey to the Falkland Islands, the only place of habitation in this part of the world.

Whilst I saw some merit in their plans, I still believed that the best course of action was to stay with the ship for I believed that she would soon be released from the ice and able to once more sail north and to safety. This I told the assembled crew with all of the earnestness and passion which I could muster.

Unhappily they were resolved to carry out their plan and urged me to come with them as their leader and navigator. I was thus torn between two emotions. My first duty was to the crew of the ship and in this I felt that my course of action was still the best chance of survival. I also had considerable faith in the strength and design of the ship to free itself from the ice. But then again, there was no foretelling what the fickle Antarctic weather would do in the next few weeks. Winter was almost upon us and the last few weeks of fall[4] would be our only chance of some warmer weather. After that, the cold blasts from the south would intensify and we would be locked here for many months until our meagre supplies would become exhausted.

I came to a fateful decision. "Very well," I said. "Perhaps you are right in this plan, but I still advise against it and suggest that those who wish it should go and those who wish to stay with me aboard the *Australis* and wait for good weather can do so."

---

[4] Autumn

There was a confused commotion as the men loudly discussed my options. When the hubbub died down, Mr Turling spoke up.

"Captain Tobey, we do not want to desert you here in this icy ship so we urge you again to take us home as our captain and leader. We are not a disloyal crew but we are resolved to quit this ship and make a positive move to head to safety. Won't you please change your mind?"

"No, I am sorry," I replied. "I must stay with my ship, but I freely allow any man to leave without any stigma of desertion. As to leadership and navigation I would trust that Mr Warren would go with you and see you all safe." With this I turned and looked at my first mate who was standing beside me as always.

"Oh, Jamie lad," he said quietly, "don't make me desert you here! Turling is possibly right in his plan and we would need you as our captain. Please come with us."

"Thank you, Caleb," I said, looking into the pleading eyes of my old friend, "but I must stay with the ship. Family pride and all that." I tried to smile and left the foc'sle with a tear in my eye.

Both officers followed me to my cabin and again urged me to go with the men for all had decided to quit the ship. Perhaps it was stubborn pride, indecision due to my youth or just plain stupidity but I confirmed my intension to stay with the ship and wait out for some later rescue, either soon, when the seas open, or at worst after the next spring thaw. There being no more to be said, the men left me to contemplate my decision to remain aboard alone.

Chapter Eleven
Alone on the Ice

Position unknown
6⁰F, high winds 20 knots from the South

Perhaps it was a faint glimmer of hope amongst the crew or perhaps a break from the ennui which had descended upon the ship along with the foul weather. Whatever the reason, the men now went about the many tasks which would enable them to leave the ship with a little more enthusiasm. The whale boats were slung out and slid down our makeshift ramp to the relative flatness of the ice floes below. I watched their exertions with some envy as I had mixed feelings about my decision and wondered whether or not I would eventually regret it. After a short time, I felt that I could not be of any use to their labours and so retired to my cabin to brood over my fate. I was soon joined by my first mate, Caleb Warren, his cap in his weather-beaten hands.

"Jaimie," he said, "won't you please reconsider coming with us? The men would be grateful for your leadership and we all feel bad about leavin' you here."

"Thankee, Caleb," I replied, touched by the personal nature of his appeal. He had long been a friend of our family and had served father for a long time and was more of a personal friend than one of my officers." I would like to go with you but I owe father the faith he put in this ship. It will survive the ice; I strongly believe and I am apprehensive about the men's chances."

"Aye. I can understand that Jaimie, but the men are resolved to look for salvation rather than risk waiting through the cold of the winter. You cannot blame them; too many of them went through the horrors of the crushing of the *Aquinnah* to remain here with the ice again pressing in."

"Yes, Caleb. I can understand that and I wish them well," I admitted.

"Jaimie…." Caleb hesitated. "I am sorry. It grieves my heart to say this, but I must go with the men also. I am your first mate and have always tried to do my best for your father and for you in this command, but the men need more leadership than that which Mr Turling can offer and Mr Dunsmuir is somewhat lost without his engine."

"Thank you, Caleb for that sentiment," I replied. "You must go with the men for here your responsibility is to the crew and not a stubborn captain." I tried to offer some light-hearted approval but he knew that my soul was not in it. "I would like you to take the spare boat compass and our spare sextant and its almanac and I will make a copy of Nathaniel Palmer's excellent chart of the waters to our northeast, for that is the way to go."

"Thankee, Cap'n," he replied and with a knuckle to his forehead, he donned his cap and left the cabin before he showed a tear.

Accordingly, I went to the chart room and selected the map drawn by the whaler Nathaniel Palmer who had explored the regions to our north some thirty years previously. There were few names as seals and not cartography was Palmer's prime concern, but the main islands and the mainland were well marked and Deception Island, our refuge those many weeks back had been both named and its position charted by Palmer. With luck, the boats should reach the warmth of this island and this should again provide some respite for the longer journey to safety. I consulted Palmer's original chart and reckoned that the distance to Deception was only about 100 nautical miles[1]. With good sailing weather this would only take about two days but this assumed open water and it may take weeks to find a lead which opened up to the sea to the north. Moreover, there was great uncertainty that this brief respite in the weather would hold for such a long haul across the ice.

My doubtful thoughts were interrupted by a brief knock at my cabin door and the entrance of Mr Dunsmuir the engineer. He saw that I was in the chart room and came in. His entrance and bluff features put shame to the sad expression on his honest face.

"Och, yer 'ere, captain? Weel a'm sorry to lea th' ship bit mist ye ken. Thare is na hawp fur us 'ere," he said in as forceful manner as he could. "Ah hae tae claise doon th' boiler, ye ken. Th' wahter in th' pipes wull freeze 'n' break

---

[1] Approximately 185 kilometres.

thaim up," he shook his head and looked away. "It wull git mighty cauld wi'oot th' steam heating th' ship ye ken?"

This was perhaps the longest conversation I had had with this tough Scot from Newfound. He continued, his broad accent becoming more excited with every word. "Bit nae tae worry yersel', laddie. Ye hae th' wee stove 'ere in yer cabil 'n' we wull bring up wood 'n' coal fae below tae keep ye warm. A'm sorry tae lea ye sae, Captain bit ah hae tae gang." With that, he quickly grasped my hand and shook it, turned and left the room as hurriedly as he had entered it.

By midday the men had completed their tasks. Lars the carpenter had used wooden slats and canvas from Ezekiel Chapman's sail-making store to fashion covers across all of the boats. These could be pulled back to allow the hoisting of the boat's sails or for rowing depending upon the sea conditions. Mr Dunsmuir's small crew and worked through the night making small stoves out of large food cans. These sat upon boxes of sand and could be used for cooking as well as heating. He also provided a good supply of coal and timber for their use. Each boat was well supplied with much preserved and canned food as was possible in the confines of such small boats and a keg of water and some spirits were also stowed in their bows. Hauling ropes had been made from our stores so that the boats could be pulled over the ice by their crews. The boats would go in three pairs with one boat of each pair going in front of the other. In open water, the plan was to have each pair tethered together by a long line so as to maintain their positions should the weather again close in; each boat having its own propulsion by sail or oar.

I came out on deck to watch as the three forlorn groups slowly hauled their boats out into the icy grey gloom which had now settled around the ship. Caleb Warren lead the first group of two boats followed by Mr Turling. He had not made any farewells with me and I had always felt that his personality was well favoured to our current climes. Joseph Turling was a young officer who always seemed to have the attitude of bored indifference; as though he was waiting for a rapid elevation to command so that he could show his current superiors that he was a better man. The third group, bringing up the rear was now commanded by Lars the carpenter; Mr Dunsmuir and his assistant engineer Stevens not being happy commanding anything which was not powered by steam.

As I watched, Lars turned and gave a broad wave with his huge arms before covering his face in his hands then turning once more to pick up the trace of his boat.

I waved back, more as a gesture of good luck than goodbye. It was only a few minutes but felt like an eternity until the boats and their pitiful teams of men disappeared into the wind-driven snow which was now swirling across the ice from the ever-present southerly wind. There was no more to be seen and so I turned and walked to my cabin.

Mr Dunsmuir's team had left a warm and cheery room far from the cold and wind that now swept the ice outside. The little box stove which stood against the wall on the port side corner of my cabin was now alight and gave a rosy glow over the entire space. At least the ship's list to port would not interfere with the opening of door. True to his word, there were also two bags of coal and a large barrel of cut pieces of timber standing nearby.

Against the adjacent wall was a sizeable stack of boxes and barrels which close inspection revealed were supplies which Jacob Simmons, the cook had brought up from the galley. There was a plentiful supply of dried meat, fish, soup, and peas as well as boxes of oatmeal, cheese, ship's biscuit, chocolate powder and tins of preserved vegetables, a box of dried potatoes, raw onions and some cases of lemons. There was also a large barrel of water and one small barrel of rum. At least I would not go hungry for a while and had enough supplies here in my cabin to last for several weeks. The thought of going down into the cold interior of the ship for these daily necessities had been an unpleasant one which I had pushed out of my mind.

Despite of these comforts supplied and the good wishes of my departed crew, the melancholy of my loneliness soon sweep upon me and I fell upon my bunk and sobbed.

It was not in my practical nature to fall into this pit of despair for long. I suddenly regained my sanity and became resolved to get on with my life and to do everything practical to keep myself from depression and to maintain my life aboard my ship.

My first task was to reorganise the chart room next door. My cabin was warm to the degree of being too hot, but beyond the bulkhead and the door leading to the chart room, the lack of heating by our faithful and efficient steam pipes meant that condensation in the air was soon precipitating on the walls and every other surface in the room. Already several small icicles were forming from the deckhead above which was a good layer of ice and snow on the roof of the deckhouse.

I gathered up all of the charts which had been left on the tables and chairs around the cabin and brushed them off with a dry cloth. They were then returned to the wide, flat drawers of the chart cabinet except for the most valued chart by Nathaniel Palmer which I would keep in the bookcase in my cabin. This took a considerable time for we had not been the tidiest of navigators. Soon the cabin was bare of any exposed material which would deteriorate in such icy conditions. The sextant and its almanac were always kept in my cabin for safe-keeping and to this collection I added the large brass telescope which had always been kept near the outer door of the chart room. It now being vary late in the day, I prepared a simple meal of reconstituted dried meat and ship's biscuit followed by a strong cup of coffee and a goodly tot of rum. I read from Palmer's journal for a short while on my bunk before I fell asleep being exhausted more by the emotional strain of the last day rather than physical exertion.

Chapter Twelve
I am not Alone

Position unknown
3⁰F, high winds 15 knots from the South

I spent a fitful night full of visions of men battling the white, snowy winds as they hauled their heavy boats across the rough ice. I awoke in a sweat despite the intense cold for the little stove had been depleted during the night. The embers were cold, and my cabin was beginning to resemble the abandoned chart room. There was a glistening of light off the ice crystals when I had lit my bedside candle and my hand had adhered to the wall where the bare skin had touched the freezing condensation of my breath. Without thinking, I had pulled my hand quickly from the wall's icy grip, leaving a little skin behind and with some haste, I threw on my heavy sea-coat and kindled the flame in the stove anew.

The day was one of anxious inactivity. Had I made the wrong decision? What had I achieved on my first command? What would be the fate of my crew or myself for that matter? Inactivity is the devil's partner and so I struggled to think of those small tasks with which I could occupy myself during the long months that may come.

My first thought was to survey the general state of the poor *Australis* so I opened the door which led directly out to the deck just behind the mainmast. I was greeted by a solid wall of ice which barred my exit. Using the small hatchet which had been left with the barrel of kindling, I attempted to cut a pathway through this ice. After making a small hole of no more than a few inches, I realised that the ice was too thick for such a puny implement. I went through the chart room to its external door which opened out to the small wheelhouse aft. Upon opening this door, I found a similar wall of ice. To get through such an ice wall I was going to need a heavier implement.

Lighting a lantern from the chart room, I went down the companion ladder which led down to the officers' dining room below deck. From here one could continue on to any part of the ship below the waterline. My passage was slow as the steps of the companion ladder were coated with an invisible, thin layer of ice as were the handrails. The dining room also sparkled in the glow of the lantern light as it too had acquired a thin coating of crystalline ice. However, as I cautiously moved further down into the dark interior of the ship, I noticed that the ice no longer coated the surfaces and the air felt slightly warmer, even though it would be well below freezing point. It was no doubt the thickness of the hull and the insulating properties of the water and thick snow above which prevented the compartments below the waterline from freezing over. Making my way forward through the galley and on to the area which contained the storerooms and coal bunkers, I reached the boson's store which contain the general spare parts and tools required by the ship. Here I found a large crowbar and a sizeable hammer which could be used in chipping through the solid ice walls which barred my way from the upper deck.

Returning to my cabin, I spent the next few hours chipping away at the ice at the main cabin door. It seemed to me a bizarre scene with the ice chips flying away in the lamplight at every stroke of my hammer. Eventually, a sudden forward motion of my crowbar and a small black space rewarded my efforts and soon I had opened a space big enough to squeeze through. It was still just afternoon, but already the light was beginning to fade and visibility across the deck was very limited. In the gloom I could see that the poor *Australis* had already been absorbed into the icy wasteland. Now it had become simply a long ridge of snow and ice; only the two masts and the edge of one of the lowered yards protruded through the top layer of powdered snow. Listing to port, the gun'le on that side had disappeared beneath the snow and so now there was a smooth, inclined slope running down to merge with the flat ice field below. My hope in freeing my poor ship of some of its white entrapment had become a labour more than that which could be accomplished by any full crew or Hercules for that matter. The wind still blew constantly from the south, the cold was bitter and so I retired once more to my cabin and closed the door.

Resigned now to my fate as a prisoner of the ice, I set about staying alive. I stoked my small stove with a good scuttle full of coal and searched my supplies for what Jacob, our cook would have called 'comfort food'. Such fare he would cook up when the men had gone through some trial or other and needed a little cheer.

"Thars nuthin' thet will raise a man's spirit like good grub!" he would say, and I guess that he was right in that respect. Inspired by such recollection, I decided to make up a pemmican stew. This recipe had been taught to me by Joseph Miantumi – a Native American of the Narragansett tribe and one of the harpooners on the *Australis*. It was an old recipe he admitted which had been passed onto his tribe by the Cree who lived further northwest and was very good for the long winter months. It consisted of a mixture of dried meat of any variety and about half as much fat. I had both in plentiful supply. My dried meat was generally beef and Jacob was never short of beef fat or dripping in his cooking. Soon there was a very pleasant smell of a bubbling stew as I stirred the mixture on my small stove; the firelight adding to the ambiance of the cabin.

To this pemmican mix I also added slightly more of the composition of ship's biscuit which I had crumbled up in my hands and a little water to make it into a porridge-like consistency. A handful dried raisons were also added for some additional flavour.[1]

I took my plate of stew, a good cup of strong black coffee and a tot of warm rum over to the small table next to my easy chair in the corner facing the stove. Despite the angle of the cabin, the chair and its foot stool were quite stable and very comfortable. After my repast and rum, I threw my

---

[1] This recipe is similar to what the early 20th century Antarctic explorers such as Scott and Shackleton would call 'Hoosh'.

rug over my feet and layed back feeling most replete. In a very short while, the tensions of the day overcame my body and I drifted off to sleep.

Suddenly I was woken out of my satisfied slumber by a loud scratching and rattling of the door which led to the chart room. I was not alone.

Chapter Thirteen
The Hunter
Position unknown
10°F, moderate winds 15 knots from the South

I was shaken by the sudden and totally unexpected rattling of my cabin door. The ship had been deserted and was now trapped in the ice many miles from any land. I knew of no threat to my safety in Antarctica save the climatic conditions, leopard seals, Orcas, the occasional angry skua and my fellow man. What abomination could be trying to gain access to my cabin in this stranded ship miles from the nearest water?

I jumped from my bunk and ran over to my desk drawer. In it I kept my pistol, an old French navy pistol which had belonged to father and who insisted that I kept it on board and loaded.

I slowly and silently walked to the door which connected to the chart room and now rattled with the force of something attempting to force it open. Grasping the handle, I was resolved to defend myself against whatever the creature may be. I slowly turned the handle and then quickly opened and pulled the door towards me, my pistol levelled and ready to fire.

A large ginger cat, its bushy tail completely upright confidently walked in the room past my bare legs. For a brief moment I just stood there watching the animal walk over and sit down in front of my small stove. My fear turned to uncontrollable joy and I sat down on the floor in fit of laughter.

It was the ship's cat which had been brought aboard by Lars the carpenter before the *Australis* had left his native Norway. Caleb Warren had remarked on the addition of this unexpected crewmember when we left New Bedford and I had lightly accepted the fact that a ship's cat would be most useful in keeping the mice and rats at bay during our expedition.

Lars had brought the cat from his parent's farm near Finse in the cold mountains of his homeland and had bragged to his shipmates in the foc'sle that the cat was a male Norsk skogkatt or Norse forest cat and so would be used to the snow and ice of Antarctica. Lars called the cat 'Jeger' which in Norse meant 'hunter' but as Lars' pronunciation of this name, which sounded something like 'yea-yid', was difficult to pronounce, the crew had nicknamed the cat Eric the Red after the famous Viking explorer, because of the cat's colour. Eric, for this was the usual abbreviation used by the crew, was a very large cat, somewhat of the proportions of a medium-sized dog. He was heavily-boned and muscular with a large triangular head and covered all over in thick fur which varied from a light to dark red-brown. He stood about eighteen inches high and was over three feet long from head to the tip of his long and very bushy tail and probably weighed around fifteen pounds[1]

Eric had rarely come aft to the officers' quarters but spent most of his time well below decks and in the comfort of the foc'sle where he was a favourite of the crew. Now he was a welcome addition to my lonely cabin and so I walked over to him and patted his soft, golden head. He turned and looked up at me with his large, golden eyes and gave a short purr of acknowledgement. I soon became aware of the old saying that one does not own a cat but is adopted as a lower member of its family.

I stoked the fire with more coal and took one of the bowls from the small crockery hutch in the cabin. This I filled with some small pieces of preserved meat which I softened with a little warm water which I had in a pot near the stove and offered it to the cat. He had no hesitation in eating this fare accompanied by more loud purring.

Eric proved to be a most welcome companion and, like a dog, would follow me around in my daily activities regardless of the cold. His paws were quite large for a cat and also covered with a thick layer of fur so that only the small pads on the soles were exposed. Always curious, he would look into every item with which I was engaged.

---

[1] Height 46 cm, length 90 cm, weight almost 7 kilograms.

I would talk to him as I would any other member of the crew and he seemed to respond accordingly. It certainly was not because of any literal understanding of my New England English, but probably my body movements, and intonation. Soon I got to recognise his different sounds and movements and we both fell into a daily routine although I am not sure as to who was training whom!

It was my practice to start the day at about six in the morning, regardless of the season and retire about ten in the evening. Eric soon became accustomed to my schedule, but as he was more accustomed to roam during the night, I would often have him jump up onto my bunk slightly earlier than my six-a.m. rising. If I did not wake to this movement, he would walk along my body with a large purr until I opened my eyes to find a large cat's face peering back at me. I would then arise, don my thick coat and present more preserved meat pieces in his bowl. Content with that, he would lay in front of the stove with a look of anticipation which suggested that it should be instantly rekindled. This I would do and the satisfied cat would then curl up and sleep for some hours.

Later, Eric would find where I was working and join me in my labours. This could mean searching through the stores well below decks or assisting with my efforts in chipping away at the wall of ice at the external door to my cabin. He would often sit with his back away from me in an alert stance as though he were keeping guard from some external predator. Around four in the afternoon, it became my habit to give Eric his second meal and it soon became the practice that he would find me at about the half hour before that time. He would stride up to where I was working and give a purposeful and long 'meow', then he would turn and walk over to the store of preserved meats if I was in the cabin, or he would walk off towards the cabin, occasionally turning to see if I had understood his command and was dutifully following. After eating, he would sit next to me whilst I dined and would pat me gently on the leg to remind me to give him his usual treat. This was a small piece of dried fish which he had become very fond of and I could always get his attention or call him in from the cold with the promise of such a treat. I would usually say:

"Eric, come here and I will give you a cat treat." At the mention of that word I would get an instant response of ears pricking up, the bushy tail rising to its vertical position and a quick rush to where I was sitting or standing. Should I sit down to my own meal first, Eric would come and sit by my side and wait for his treat. That not being forthcoming, he would gently tap me on the leg with his left paw until such times as a treat was given.

Retiring to my cabin and sitting in my easy chair with a good book was the usual signal for Eric to jump up on my lap and demand some grooming. Once satisfied, he would move about until comfortable and then settle down, coiled up with his nose covered by his tail and fall asleep. This was easily interrupted by any change in the sounds around the cabin or any slight movement on my part. When it was my time to sleep, he would jump off and wait in front of the stove to remind me that it required more coal. Usually a few minutes after I had extinguished the candle next to my bunk, he would jump up onto the end of the quilt and curl up for a few hours until he went off on his usual nocturnal inspections.

True to his name, Eric the hunter would sometimes bring me a sample of his hunting prowess. This was accompanied by a loud series of urgent 'meows' which I had initially though was a cry of pain but was in fact a cry for assistance. Eric's prey would be in the form of a small mouse or rat which he would bring to the cabin and deposit it on the floor at the foot of my bunk. I had cut a small doorway in the base of the cabin door which led to the Chart Room which would give him access to the rest of the ship below decks. This small opening, I had covered with a strip of leather to keep out some of the cold but to allow Eric to come and go. On most occasions his prey, which was brought to me no doubt as a contribution to my food store, was usually alive. This was not welcome as I often had to get up and recapture the small quarry as it escaped from Eric's paws.

I had assumed that all of the rodents onboard the *Australis* had left the ship before we had sailed south from the Falklands or had died below in the cold, dark regions of the hull. Somehow some had survived and had become the natural prey of the ship's cat. My previous solitude had softened my heart to any creature which could live in such cold conditions, so I would accept Eric's donation and reward him with a fish treat. The mouse or rat I would take below and release it to go back to its normal abode.

Later on, I was to find that Eric was also a very brave cat as well as a great hunter. Having cleared the ice from the external door to my cabin, I was determined to have some freedom and go fishing to improve my diet of dried meat with some fresh fish. Father had often taken me to the lakes north of New Bedford for winter fishing, especially after pike. We would carefully walk across the frozen waters of Long Pond and cut a small hole with our saw. If the wind was blowing, we would often erect our canvas wind break and sit for hours trying to keep warm whilst the fish below decided whether or not to take our lure.

Accordingly, I gathered together what I needed, for there were plenty of lines in the foc'sle and preserved fish for bait and a saw and spade would be needed to make a hole in the ice. The ice flow which surrounded the ship consisted of a jigsaw pattern of ice covered over with several feet of new snow. I would take a long boathook with which to probe the snow for a weakness between the floes and there I would attempt to cut my fishing hole.

Eric the Red

The Leopard seal

I carefully walked down the portside slope of snow and carefully made my way around the hull so as not venture too far from the ship; just far enough to get away from the piled jumble that held its hull. With the wind still blowing, I built a small wall of packed snow behind which I could shelter and cut my hole. After some hours, I finally succeeded in cutting a large round hole about three feet across. I put down the piece of carpet which I had brought with me and upon it placed my gear and small stool which I had found in the galley. Naturally Eric had followed me and had found a comfortable piece of carpet under the stool. Luck was not with us that day and so after a few cold hours with the light fading even further, I decided to retreat to my cabin and try again tomorrow.

On the next day, late in the morning, we again headed out over the ice to our fishing hole. I rounded the snow wall, which protected our fishing hole to be greeted with a loud, gruff open-mouth roar of a Leopard seal which had used our fishing hole as an air hole or what the Inuit called an aglus. Taken back by this unexpected confrontation, I stepped back and tripped on a raised patch of ice. With the fearsome seal lumbering towards me, I had a brief glimpse of an orange body flashing past with a loud, high-pitched scream. It was Eric going into the attack and swiping the seal across its snout with his claws. With a strange yelp, the Leopard seal turned quickly and dove into the fishing hole and disappeared. Eric stood on the edge of the ice quivering and shuddering his jaws in a low chorus of defiance. I quickly got to my feet, and picking Eric up into my arms walked as fast as I could across the snow to the safety of the *Australis*.

Chapter Fourteen
The Mysterious Light

Latitude 64° 2' 37' South, Longitude 62° 39' 53" West
12⁰F, light winds 10 knots from the West

As the days wore on, I decided that enduring the cold very early in the morning when the fire in my small stove had almost extinguished was not the most desirable of comforts, so Eric and I moved below decks to the galley. Here was a larger ship's oven which, despite the angle of the deck was still quite useable. Moreover, the coal bunkers and the wood of the carpentry shop was just next door. Jacob Simmons our cook, being an Old Salt, had rigged his hammock in an alcove between the bulkheads facing the oven. I made up a comfortable bed for Eric out of an old box and a woollen blanket. Cats seem to like the confines of a box and so he was very happy with the arrangement although he was initially frustrated that I was now above ground in my new hammock and well away from his early morning wake-up walks.

I spent the next few days carrying my supplies and books from the upper cabin down through the chart room. Eric was initially unsure of these actions as cats are ultra-conservatives and always become suspicious of any change. Throughout the entire process, Eric was not too far behind me on my trips between cabin and galley. Eventually he accepted our new home, especially when I relit the galley fire and made us both an excellent supper. By stoking the oven firebox with a goodly supply of coal before turning in, I was able to keep the oven lit all night with just some additional coal upon the hot coals the next morning to get the fires back to a good heat. In addition, there was now a plentiful supply of hot water because of the cast-iron water tank which had been fixed to the upper surface of the oven. Life was becoming more comfortable. Here too was an opportunity to have the luxury of a bath. Previously my bath, an elongated zinc-plated tub would be brought to my sleeping cabin and filled with water by my cabin boy, Thomas who would later empty it using a bucket. This bath now stood in the small store just off the galley and there was a plentiful supply of hot water in the cistern attached to the galley stove. For my ablutions, I had made up a small water closet of sorts in a disused store further forward. This consisted of a wide bucket covered with two wooden slats. After use, I would add a little water and then the next morning would throw the contents overboard.

One night, or perhaps I should say late one afternoon for the faint sunlight had completely given way to the blackness of night, I went back up to my old cabin to retrieve an old journal which I had need to consult. Upon entering the cabin from the chart room, I had the uncomfortable feeling that something was not just right. To be sure, my cabin had become like the chart room and now had walls shining with crystalline ice in the small light of my lantern but there was something else. I stood for a moment and tried to collect all of my senses. The cabin was still in the same condition in which I had left it in my retirement to the galley; the books; journals and maps were all secured in the book case and the floor and bunch were clear of anything unusual. It was then that I realised what was wrong! The incessant noise of the wind whistling or shrieking through the standing rigging was absent!

With some excitement I opened the external door and quickly pushed away the wall of recent snow using the old coal scuttle belonging to my small stove. I broke through the white mass into complete darkness. Venturing out onto the slippery deck, I was confronted with a warm calm and above me the myriad twinkling of thousands of stars. The wind had completely dropped and with it the air temperature felt warmer than the perpetual cold which my men and I had endured for weeks. The fog and low cloud had completely disappeared and now presented a perfectly clear sky of stars and light of a half-moon shining in the northern sky.

What a glorious feeling to be free of the southerly blast which had brought a premature winter down to entrap my ship. I climbed up onto the high mound of the snow-covered deck house to survey my surroundings. To the west and south there was an endless vista of white ice fading out into a vague horizon. I turned to take in the scene to the east and was shocked at what I saw.

There was the usual scene of white disappearing into the darkness, but at some great distance beyond that was a single, faint light. What could it be? Who would have a light in this vast wilderness? Surely not another ship for there was only one single light with the usual side lights of red and green?

I dashed back into the cabin where I had kept a small personal hand compass in my desk drawer. It was a very expensive brass instrument which my father had given to me when I first went to sea. It was not as elaborate as a portable boat compass which Mr Warren had taken for his navigation, but a personal item for my own use in places away from home. I took it and went back up to my snowy observation point. Taking a sighting through the upright rear sight, I found that the strange light was bearing approximately110^0 magnetic; a little south of east. I carefully noted my standing position on the roof of the deck house and then returned to the cabin to retrieve the spare sextant from the chart room. Returning to the deck, I soon found the constellation of Crux, or the Southern Cross at a high angle above me. Acrux was the brightest star in this constellation and featured in my almanac of astronavigation. This was never my strong point, and the horizon was still only a blur but I took a fix on the star and several others which I remembered from my navigation lessons which had until this time been confined only to the Northern Hemisphere. I now could estimate my position from these sightings and the good reliable chronometer which still worked despite the cold. By consulting the almanac for the date and using the sightings and the local time compared to that of Greenwich which had zero degrees of longitude, I found that my approximate position was 64° 2' 37' South latitude and 62° 39' 53'' West longitude. During the last few weeks, the pack ice and my ship within it had drifted some fifteen nautical miles to the northwest.

Hurriedly, I went back down to the galley where I had taken my most precious charts and found the map and journal of Nathaniel Palmer. I plotted my position on his old map and found that I was now close inshore of the big island which we had rounded that fateful day when our propeller had broken. From the bearing which I had taken, the mysterious light appeared to be coming from the large promontory on the north-western side of that island. Using the scale of the map, I estimated that the shoreline should be no more than about eight nautical miles from my present position and I became resolved to look for the source of that light; but that would have to wait until daylight tomorrow.

In the meantime, I needed to make some preparations and I was excited of the prospect of solving the mystery before me. My ventures onto the icepack had proven that good sea boots were not well suited for the slippery surface ice nor deep, soft snow. Lars had kept a set of Nordic skis in his carpentry store but I had never learned how to use such implements. I remembered how the Native People and early trappers had made snowshoes to traverse the snowy wilderness and set about making myself a set. Lars had a plentiful supply of long, thin battens of wood in his carpentry store. These were used as strengthening battens in the sails of our whaleboats and were flexible enough to be bent around to form a tear-drop shape of about three feet long which could be used to make my snowshoes. Having bent the timber around to the basic shape, I then used more battens to weave a basket-like pattern over their surface. These I held in place by some good sailor knots and some gum Arabic which I found in the store. An old pair of sea boots were attached to the centres of these frames and so my snowshoes were ready for the morning. Eric sat by attentively watching my efforts but I detected some apprehension on his part. Where was I going?

Chapter Fifteen
The Ice Cave

Latitude 64° 3' 12' 'South, Longitude 62° 34' 00" West
20⁰F, light winds 5 knots from the West

My preparations continued during the night. I had found an old seaman's kit bag in the store which had a rope which could be looped from the open draw-string to its base and so could be carried over the shoulder and across the back. This I loaded with a good quantity of dried pemmican which I had previous made and stored in my old 'icebox' sleeping cabin, blocks of chocolate and dried fruit, some raw potatoes, onions, a small pot and my old coffee pot which contained a small bag of ground beans and another small bag of sugar. I also had followed the idea of the cook and had made a small stove from an empty can which had air holes punched around its sides near its base. Spare socks and an extra warm jacket went next and a large length of canvas to act as a tent and my spare oilskins followed.

I found a good boat hook which was about six feet in length and tightly lashed another of the same size to it. Apart from being a good stave when walking, these two poles could be embedded into the snow as tent poles. A small spade for digging snow was lashed to the outside of the kit bag. These were also the centre rod for a bundle of light timber which I would use as fuel to supplement the bottle of paraffin[1] carefully stowed away in the bag. Two round water

---

[1] Kerosene

canteens, the type often used by prospectors and sometimes taken on the whaleboats as extra water supplies, completed my load. These canteens I would fill with hot water from my stove before setting out. I would carry them over my shoulders, one on each side beneath my coat and so they would provide some extra warmth as well as the water's not freezing in the cold air.

My faithful Eric had sat watching these proceedings with some agitation. He suspected that I would be leaving the ship and his company. Cats seem to understand when there were to be major changes in their social habits. I estimated that I would be no more than two days absent so I placed extra food out in the galley for Eric in several large bowls. Water too, was placed in several large containers shallow enough for him to reach but wide enough to give a copious volume. I would stoke the oven with extra coal and several large pieces of hardwood to ensure that the fire would burn for at least most of my absence.

After a short fitful sleep, as I was eager to start my journey, I awoke and set about preparing for my trip at the first glimmer of sunlight. It was well into the morning when I carried my bag up through my old sleeping cabin and out onto the deck. The wind was still blowing from the west but not as strong as the day before. There was a faint glow to the east but visibility was again reduced to only a few yards.

Never-the-less, I patted Eric who had dutifully followed me up onto the deck and reassured him that I would be back. It seemed strange to talk thus to a cat but I felt somehow that he would understand. Pushing the toes of my sea boots into my new snowshoes and shouldering my bag, I took firm hold of my staff and began the descent down the snow ramp which led onto the icepack. Now on the relatively flat surface beyond the jumble of ice and snow which surrounded the ship. I turned back and waved to Eric who stood stoically on the heaped snow of the aft deckhouse.

"I'll be back!" I called, trusting that the brave cat would understand something of the meaning. He was an intelligent animal and I hoped that he would soon tire of the cold and go below. I trudged off into the white haze, closely following the compass bearing which I had taken the night before.

At first my progress was good. I soon got into a routine of thrusting my staff into the snow to sound for weak spots which would indicate an open crevasse then, finding the ice to be solid under the snow I would take another step. After a while I came up to my first obstacle, a pressure ridge. This was where separate ice floes had collided and continued to push together until one slide up over the other. Sometimes both were pushed up into a steep wall which ran off into the snow haze in both directions. All of this was usually covered in a thick cover of snow. If the snow was very thick it would form a gentler slope up which I could slowly climb. Sometimes the wind had blown much of the snow away and so a steep, broken ridge of ice would be my barrier. Such walls were hard to climb as I had soon found that snowshoes did not afford much traction on ice. I would have to make a series of small, flat steps into the icy slopes using the spade which I carried on my back. Soon my method of walking became careful steps with my staff in one hand and the spade in the other. Thus equipped, I slowly made small progress along my bearing. Unfortunately, without much visibility and no distant object on which to sight, I had to watch my bearing constantly as well as to look to keep my footing.

My trek over the icefield was taking much longer than I had imagined with the smoothness of the ice being very deceptive. Where the ice floes were large and covered with a good layer of fresh snow, I made good progress but occasional failures in the snow bridges over places where the floes had moved apart were both common and dangerous. After a few hours, I was comforted by an increase in visibility. The faint sunlight now penetrated more of the mist which had descended over the icefield and I could see for at least one hundred yards.

Eventually I perceived through the mist the raised outline of the coastal edge of the island. There were many steep sections where the snow had not covered and these now stood out as dark grey rocky outcrops. I checked my compass and confirmed that I was still marching on my correct bearing. Stopping, I wiped the snow from my face and attempted to look towards where that mysterious light should be. There was a faint movement a little to the left and on concentrating my vision I saw that it was a small group of men moving about down near the edge of the shore. Here the ice had also piled up, but currents within the water below ensured that there was a gap of open water between the ice field and the mainland. I marched on determined to make myself known as soon as I could; the wind permitting.

After a few more paces, I saw that one of the men had climbed up onto the ice field and was waving his hands and pointing in my direction. They had seen me! The man climbed over the jumble of ice and now ran towards me with an occasional stumble on the smooth ice. It was easy to recognise the tall figure of Lars the carpenter who now took of his cap and waved frantically at me, his shouts being blown away in the wind. His long blonde hair streamed in the wind as he ran towards me. The other men, too had now climbed up onto the ice and were waving their hands and caps in excitement.

Lars came up to me in a very uncertain gait as he was having trouble keeping his footing in the snow and ice and also was uncertain who this stranger might be. At last he realised who I was.

"Kaptein, Herregud er det du![2] He said with so much excitement he had lapsed into his native Norwegian.

---

[2] "Captain, my God it is you!"

"Yes, Lars. It is I," I replied, there being nothing else I could say as I too was astonished at this meeting.

The big Norwegian ran forward and grabbed me around and lifted me bodily off the snow.

"Oh! I hav gludness to see ya, Kaptein!" he cried, putting me down and standing back to ensure that his eyes had not played tricks upon him and that I was flesh and blood and not some apparition coming out of the mist. "Komme, ve go see tha men, ja?" and he turned and strode off.

By now the men who had been standing on the snow now formed a tight group up on one of the snow-covered ice slabs and were most excited, jumping up and waving their caps with cries of "It's the Captain!" and "salvation at last!" Soon I was surrounded with the happy faces of the men pressed into see that this figure really was their lost Captain.

Looking around at the group of blackened, weather-beaten faces I recognised some of the true and trusted hands; Krystof the hardy Pole, Taumalolo, the Islander harpooner, Tobias Henry our quartermaster, Seamus O'Leary one of our stokers and young Thomas Dillon my cabin boy. Looking around I said "but Lars, where are the rest of your men? There are only six here. There should be twelve!"

"Kom nå til Lar sted[3]," cried the excited Lars who had once more lapsed into his native tongue and as one group we followed the big man along the shore line to a large snow drift which reached up against a rocky headland high above us. At its base was a small hole; no more than about five feet square which seemed to go down into the drift. Lars ducked his head and went down through the hole. I and the rest of the men followed in turn through the hole.

The short entrance tunnel went firstly down into a wide, ice-filled pit and then turned sharply upwards, opening out into a large space. It was, at first sight like something that my lovely Liv had once read to me on one of our pleasant evenings at the home of her father, that brilliant shipwright Peder Andersen in Bergen. Here she had read to me some stories of the myths of her homeland[4] about the Trolls who lived under the mountain in great halls where they would dance and feast all day waiting for nightfall.

I looked about me in wonder. It was a huge snow cave, its curved, hand-smoothed sides glistening with ice crystals which reflected a dull red glow given off by the small stove which sat on a cairn of rocks in its centre. Lars explained that a large cave had been cut out of the compacted snow and into the slope of the snow drift. It was cut downwards

---

[3] "Come now to Lar's place"

[4] Probably the *Norske Folkeeventyr* (*Norwegian Fairytales*), a collection of Norwegian folktales and legends by Peter Christen Asbjørnsen and Jørgen Moe which had first appeared a slim pamphlet in 1841. The *Peer Gynt* suite by Edvard Grieg is also based upon some of these tales.

initially to provide a trap into which any meltwater would flow and turn to ice. Then the hollow was widened as a dome-like structure with a circular space in the middle and a wide ledge cut around the sides. A small channel was cut where these ledges came out of the wall and the surface of the ceiling was smoothed out by hand so that melting water would not drip from any projections. Using an oar, two holes were then pushed up through the roof of the cave; one near where the entrance would be and another over the central space where the cairn of rocks were built. These holes allowed for some fresh air to enter through one and stale air and fumes from the stove to exit through the other. A most ingenious living space. Finally, the large opening at the front was sealed up using blocks of ice which Lars had cut with a saw from the icefield and plastered with fresh snow leaving only a small entrance which could also be closed with another block of ice. As I entered, I noticed that around the walls on the ledge sat the rest of Lar's team. One man was asleep in his sleeping bag but the others now sat erect, alerted by the excited sounds outside and now completely agog at my sudden appearance.

After the initial excitement had died down, I produced the coffee pot and its supplies and bade Lars to put it onto the small stove. Whilst the coffee was brewing, Lars told me his tale and how they had come to this place. He was excited and waved his big arms around whilst he spoke in his heavily-accented English. His party was the last to leave the *Australis* those many weeks ago, but after two days of hard march pulling their two boats, they lost sight of the second party ahead of them commanded by Mr Turling. A sudden change of wind from the south had brought a fierce blizzard which gave a complete white out; a condition when the air is completely filled with driven snow and visibility is reduced to zero. Gathering his men together and making lifelines which attached each man to one of the boats, he had foolishly pressed on hoping to catch up with the next party. It was too much to endure and so after a while, with no contact being made and no answer to their calls, they pushed both boats together and sheltered below their canvas covers. It was not until the morning of the next day that the wind again swung around to the west and abated. When they emerged from below the snow-covered canvas, they saw that they were alone and surrounded by nothing but a white landscape disappearing into a white mist. Without hope of continuing their journey north without a compass, Lars, with the experience of such conditions in the mountains of his native Norway, decided to walk into the dim light which herald the faint easterly sun. He knew that the big island was somewhere to their east and that might provide some shelter and its coastline a guide to resume their course.

They had eventually found the shoreline of the island but by now the men were very weak by their exertions in hauling the two boats across the ice field with its pressure ridges and crevasses. One man, Levi Samuels, had fallen into a small crevasse but was saved by his companions but not before being immersed in the icy water up to his waist. Lars had had him stripped naked, rolled in the snow and then wrapped in borrowed clothes and a blanket and safely placed into the covered bow of the lead whaleboat. Another man, our faithful old hand Seth Rowlings, had lost his gloves in the blizzard and, saying nothing he had continued in his place on the haul lines and his fingers had become affected with frost bite. It was Levi Samuels who lay asleep in his sleeping bag throughout this animated tale.

After Lars had finished his story and his men praising him for his actions, another man whom I had not recognised as one of our Stokers, Seamus O'Leary because of the change which had been wrought upon all of their faces by their hard journey across the wind-swept icefield spoke up.

"It 'mm being a gud thang that you came whin ya did, Cap'n, darlin'. We was getting tha boat ready ta shove orf up north."

Lars explained that he was ready to continue dragging the last whaleboat back onto the ice with the six fit men leaving the others in the ice cave with most of the supplies. The other whale boat had suffered some damage in sliding across the icefield and had been broken up to cover the ledge inside the snow cave as well as to provide extra strengthening for the second boat and additional fuel for the small stoves. He had hoped to make a last-ditch effort to reach the open sea and perhaps find help from some other whaling ship, although this would be almost an impossibility in these latitudes.

"Well!" I said. "It was most fortuitous that I arrived when I did. The *Australis* is the whale ship you need and she lies just a few miles to our west. May I suggest that as darkness will be upon us in a short while that we stay here in this warm ice cave and make ready for our trip back to the ship at first light tomorrow?"

The men seemed happy at this suggestion and Lars was relieved at both the thought of returning to the warmth and security of the ship as well as handing on his responsibility of leadership to me. With agreement to that plan concluded, we poured out the hot coffee and passed it around in the few mugs which were available.

Chapter Sixteen
Redemption and Resurrection
Latitude 63° 57' 51" South, Longitude 62° 48' 28" West
25⁰F, light winds 5 knots from the West

It was good to be back in the company of my fellow man. The night was one of amiable companionship albeit with the smell of many men who had not washed for weeks and the occasional snoring of those who could sleep under any harsh condition. My sleeping bag was wet but still warmed by my body heat and so I was able to sleep for a few hours.

The fire in the small stove still flickered as Lars had set up a roster of watch-keeping so that it was kept alight. The air in the cave was cold but nothing like that outside but more akin to those temperatures which many of these New Englanders were used to at home. There was a slight blue glow through the ice at the entrance to the cave which heralded mid-morning daylight.

Lars and a few of the men had already dressed and left the cave to make ready the surviving whaleboat. The other finally awoke with the sound of movement in the cave. Gradually and painfully, the men shifted their gear down to the boat. The two injured men were carefully placed into the covered bow and the various items of useful stores loaded into the boat. It was a difficult task getting the boat through the jumble of ice, rock and water that now formed the shoreline and I was both pleasantly surprized and alarmed at the change in the weather. The wind now had returned to the west and was now reduced to a gentle breeze. The cloud was now well above the surface of the ice with the occasional patch of blue sky just showing through.

Our trip back to the *Australis* was not an easy one. The surface snow was beginning to melt and provided extra friction on the hull of our boat thus making haulage much more difficult. Nevertheless, the men were happy and hauled away with a will. One of them took up an old halyard song greatly modified for the occasion. The solo man would sing a line and the rest, as was the custom when hauling up the yard arms, would join in the well-known chorus:

SOLO: *The captain's a terrier and so it may be*
CHORUS: *Way, hey! Haul away now*
SOLO: *He's come to take us back to the sea*
CHORUS: *Haul away, haul away, Haul away now*

SOLO: *The boat is a running free on the snow*
CHORUS: *Way, hey! Haul away now*
SOLO: *It's better this way than havin' to row*
CHORUS: *Haul away, haul away, Haul away now*

SOLO: *The carpenter saved us from dyin' of cold*
CHORUS: *Way, hey! Haul away now*
SOLO: *Whoever said we'd never get old?*
CHORUS: *Haul away, haul away, Haul away now*

SOLO: *Back to our ship and safe we will be*
CHORUS: *Way, hey! Haul away now*
SOLO: *We'll get her out and head for the sea*
CHORUS: *Haul away, haul away, Haul away now*

And so, the shanty went on; a different man would sing a solo line, usually about one of their shipmates, the ship or the sea in general and the rest would join in at the chorus. Often the solo part was either humorous or bawdy and there was much laughter.

It was comforting to hear the men sing and laugh at the improvised lines, but I was apprehensive that their good spirits may soon be dashed. The wind had dropped and the temperature had risen. This in itself was a good sign to the men, but there was still a chance that the ice would open up before us and cut us off from the ship. To be sure, we had a good sea-worthy boat with us, but it was designed for no more than five or six men. Thirteen may be too many, especially if the southerly storms appeared. Moreover, they would be disappointed upon their return to the ship. It was still their icy prison trapped here at the end of the Earth.

Still, we pushed on with enthusiasm, with Lars and myself in the lead. Lars was carrying one of the long boathooks and he would march along the compass bearing which I indicated with my hand and search for any weaknesses in the ice. After about twenty yards he would stop and turn around to see if he needed to move port or starboard to be in line with my bearing. Once this was set, we would all haul up to his position and so he would continue on to the next leg. When we came to a pressure ridge, it was all hands to the boat so that was both pushed and hauled up over the slabs of ice. Sometimes the men would have to cut a pathway through the more stubborn ridges but at other times we hauled the boat over like it was going over an shoreline breaker.

After many hours of struggling across the ice and with the sun now low on the horizon we approach the *Australis*. At first the men did not see the ship for they had left her as a recognisable auxiliary steam whaler, but now she was just another raised mound of snow and ice only discernible as something different by the two masts and smoke stack sticking through the snow. The party stopped and the men dropped the traces and stood dumfounded at the long, white shape before them. Now realisation set in; they had replaced one ice abode for another, but at lease this one offered more comfort and whilst it was a poor homecoming, the ship was their home still. Suddenly Lars let out a cry:

"Jeger, min nydelige katt! Det er deg?"[1] and climbed up the steep slope of snow covering the starboard gun'le to where the little figure of Eric stood patiently. The faithful animal had been waiting for us to return and had heard our approach and come up on deck. The cat stalked over to his owner with an expression which could only mean 'where

---

[1] "Hunter. You lovely cat! It is you?"

have you been? Explain!'. Lars picked up his cat and brought him back and placed him into the whaleboat where he was welcomed and patted by our two injured men. The others quickly gathered round happily talking and wanting to pat the faithful cat who had waited this long to reclaim his owner.

Taking up the ropes again, the men followed Lars and I around to the port side of the ship where we climbed up the steep ramp of snow and onto what had once been a wooden deck. The men looked around them as though they needed to think hard about where the familiar features of the deck and cabins had been. Lars led the way by taking his shovel from the boat and starting to dig a trench to the door of the foc'sle. The rest of the men took heart and helped to clear the snow away from the door and then helping their injured comrades into the safety of their former home.

Compared to the devastation and chaos outside, the interior of the foc'sle was a haven of normality and had remained very much like what it had been when the men had left it those many weeks ago. The walls glistened with ice crystals but these were soon wiped down once the small stove in the centre of the cabin was lit. Men reclaimed their old hammocks spaces with some cheer as they had been their own small piece of safety and security. Lars and I left them to their work of restoring the foc'sle and going about getting some hot food.

The next morning, whilst I was in my old galley retreat packing up my personal belongings to return to my own cabin, I was approached by Seamus O'Leary one of our stokers.

"Beggin' yer pardon Captain, but oi tink dat oi can fire up de boiler for sum 'ayte," he said, his cap in hand and an ernest expression on his broad Irish face. "Mr Dunsmuir lef 'er in gran' order an' oi cannot fend any banjacked lines. It shud work gran', nigh".

This was great news! With steam in the boiler we could operate the steam heaters in the cabins and give some extra warmth to the ship. What was more important is that we could set up the steam hoses and clear the clinging snow and ice from the deck and sides of the ship.
"Thankee, Mr O'Leary." I replied with good humour. "You are now promoted to temporary engineer, so see to it if you please. The grinning stoker knuckled his forehead and went off calling to some of his shipmates to gather wood, paraffin and coal to relight our boiler. I turned to Lars who also beamed with some pleasure.

"Lars, be so good as to organise the men when they have eaten to start shovelling the snow and ice off our decks." I said, feeling embarrassed that I had never really knew the big carpenter's surname. "Have them search out the steam hose outlets on the deck ready to fit the hoses…oh! and have some men break them out from the store."

It took several hours for stoker O'Leary to fill the boiler tank with meltwater and to make the appropriate adjustments to the various valves and air intakes of the boiler. Soon the happy gurgle of steam passing through the heating tubes and radiators could be heard in cabins and around the ship. The men had worked incessantly cutting away the ice and shovelling the snow which had covered the decks and cabin roofs. The stream hoses were brought up from the store and attached to the outlets which had finally been exposed. Extreme caution was required with these steam hoses as a blast of steam would kill a man should he get in the way. So, it was left to two teams to play the hoses; one working from the bow to the stern along the deck, and the other being played down our snowy ramp to free the platform which had formed its base. The rest of the crew who were not working below stood off, mostly atop the roof of the foc'sle to watch the two-man team working the steam jet methodically across the deck. It was an amazing thing to watch as the steam jet made short work of the ice and snow which had piled up across the deck. Each pass of the jet cut huge swathes into the ice.

Meanwhile, the team who had taken a hose down the port side ramp had started from the deck and had slowly walked down the ramp. They too revelled in the power of the steam to remove large amounts of ice and snow. More as a jest rather than a commanded intention, this team had played the steam jet along the hull and soon found that it cleared large volumes of the distorted ice slabs which had been pushed up along with the ship. With encouragement from the men on the foc'sle roof, they continued playing the steam jet along the outer hull until it was cleared entirely of block ice right down to the normal level of the pack ice. A sudden vibration threw some of the men standing upon the roof to their knees and the men handling the steam hose had to hold fast onto a cleared section of the gun'le. The ship had been partly freed and had settled slightly, the angle of the deck almost returning almost to the horizontal position. Surprised and elated about this event, both steam hose crews now played their jets along the hull on both the port and starboard sides.

I had come up on deck to find out what had caused the vibration which had passed through the ship. So did the men who were working below and now stood up on the foc'sle roof. From my vantage point on the aft cabin roof I could clearly see the effects of the steam jets on the ice. They were at last freeing the ship of its icy shackles and soon one could see clear water around the waterline of the ship.

What an agreeable term, 'waterline'! We had not seen a true waterline for all of these long weeks and it was a joy to have the *Australis* once more floating free of the ice. Unfortunately, my smug musing did not last for long, for lifting my eyes up to the horizon, now clear of mist, I saw that we were still only in a small lake of clear water surrounded still by the immense icefield which stretched away in all directions. My heart fell at the thought that despite our hard work and the promise of modern engineering, we were still trapped in the ice.

As if to answer my prayers there was a sharp call from the crow's nest where our irrepressible cabin boy, Thomas Dillon had climbed to get a better view of the ice pack. "Blue water, ho!" he cried. This call brought all of the men on deck to the ratlines which they eagerly climbed to also get a view.

"Where away?" I called from vantage point on the cabin roof.

"Over yonder, sir." He cried, pointing a little off our port bow. North! The ice was beginning to open up now that there had been a respite from the cold southerly winds which had brought an early winter to this part of Antarctica. Perhaps we had a chance at last but it would be slim one. Still at the end of fall with light winds blowing from the west and northwest we had a chance that some leads would open up to the ship's small lake and we would be able to again make sail.

The daylight faded and so did the new hope of the men that we would soon be free. There had been no change in the icefield but through my telescope from the maintop I did see a sizeable patch of blue water to our north.

The next morning when daylight finally came, we again had clear visibility and many a man would clamber up to the yards to see if there had been any change in the ice. And there was! A long lead of blue water and opened up across our bow at about one hundred yards distant but it had continued on south, past the ship. I called all hands and pointed out our dilemma. There was open water but well away from our position. If we could only encourage the ice to split in our direction, we may have a change of freedom.

Under the enthusiastic leadership of Lars, we all took whatever implement we could and headed off towards this southerly lead. Going was slowly because there may be more crevasses under the snow and finding one of these heading towards the ship would be to our advantage. There were several small cracks going in the direction of our ship but all of them resisted our efforts to make them wide. After many hours of hard work with crowbar, axe and spade, we had opened up a small tributary of the main lead which we had hoped would crack open and connect with the ships position. Unfortunately, this crack in the ice refused to open any further. As well, the temperature was again dropping and the water in the main lead was taking on that greasy appearance of new ice forming on the water's surface. Our hopes were again dashed by the thought that the main lead would again close up with ice and our puny branch would be of no avail.

"A few shots o' a cannon would 'ave us free!" exclaimed my young cabin boy who was often prone to much imagination. The poor *Australis* was not a war ship and had no cannon. But wait! Young Thomas' idea was not a silly one at all. The kegs of gunpowder from the beached whaler on the other side of the island were still in our store.

"Quick!" I cried out to Krystof who was working nearby. "Take five men and go to the Number 4 store. You will find some small barrels marked 'gunpowder'. Bring them here as fast as you can but mind how you walk on the ice. I don't want to lose any of the barrels – and bring a bolt of canvas and a barrel of paraffin". The men laughed at my jest and, dropping their tools, Krystof and his five companions hurried back to the ship.

One hundred yards over an icefield takes a considerable time of cautious walking. More so if one is carrying a heavy barrel on one's shoulders. Upon their return, I explained to the men that I intended to blast our small man-made lead open and hope that it would continue cracking up to the ship.

One barrel was inserted firmly down into a hole at the end of our small lead. Three more were placed at about twenty-five paces along a line of weakness we had found back towards the ship. Long lengths of fuse were made by rolling a thin pouring of gunpowder along a piece of old canvas which had been also been brought from the ship and cut into long lengths. These were placed into the bung holes of each barrel so that each barrel was connected, in line to the others. The first barrel, near the main lead was to be the first to explode. Another fuse was inserted into this first barrel to run across the fresh snow for about three yards. Paraffin which was used in our lamps, was poured along this first fuse to encourage burning. I had Lars walk back along the fuse line with the paraffin barrel to soak the other fuses in a similar manner.

"Back to the ship, men and to your prayers." I commanded. "For I am about to light the main fuse so get clear as quickly as you can." The men took my meaning clear enough and headed back towards the ship as fast as they could move. Lars stayed behind to see to my safety but I suggested that one fool here was enough, so he too turned and reluctantly headed back to the ship.

When I saw that Lars and the men were a good distance off, I took my flint and steel to the end of the first fuse. It seemed rather short now that I was to light it, but I hoped that it would burn slowly enough to allow my escape. Perhaps it was the cold and strain of command which had addled my thinking. I then realised that I would have to race the entire length of the burning fuses to the other barrels back to the ship. Well! Too late now and I lit the first fuse and started back to the ship as fast as my sea boots would allow on the slippery ice.

As I half ran and half slipped my way back towards the second barrel I thought of all the things which could go wrong with my plan; would the first fuse ignite the first barrel, would that blast or the others snuff out the fuse along the way, and would the force of these blasts crack open the ice at all.

I manage to get past the second barrel when the explosion threw me off my feet. I sat up and looked at the great cloud of ice and snow falling about where the first barrel had been. I also notice the tell-tail glow of the next fuse burning towards me. I got to my feet and again ran and slide as fast as I could back towards the boat. There was another explosion but this time I was able to stay upright. I ran because my life and that of my men depended on me, their only navigator to reach the ship. Behind me I heard another explosion and as I passed the fourth barrel, I knew that the burning fuse was not far behind. The last explosion threw me up against a small snow drift where I lay for a short while, mentally and physically exhausted. Hands were reaching up under my arms and legs as Lars and Kristof carried me back to the ship.

The men were cheering and I felt an embarrassed sense of elation. This was no heroics. This was an act of intuitive survival. My embarrassment disappeared when I realised that the men were looking out from the ship and not concerned with my current welfare. I climbed to my feet and followed their outstretched arms. Sure enough, our small cut lead had cracked open along a very jagged series of natural cracks. They were only a few feet across and liable to close at any moment so I quickly gave the order to raise the jibs and the spanker and steer the ship along our new pathway.

Luckily, I had ordered the men to bend on two of our jibs at the bow and to free and make ready the large fore-an-aft spanker sail at our mainmast. We were underway at last; but only just, as the winds were still slight and coming slightly across our bow and so we would have to tack[2]. We gained some impetus immediately and so our strong, ice-strengthen bow would rise up and crack the ice every time we went about. Soon we were in the main lead and could turn north towards the open water beyond.

----

[2] When sailing into the wind, ships would have to tack or sail across the wind direction by several changes in direction. Jibs and fore-and-aft sails could do this better than square sails.

Latitude 62° 58' 37" South, Longitude 60° 39' 00" West
20⁰F, moderate winds 15 knots from the South

Before they had left the *Australis,* my officers and I had agreed that they would head north across the ice until they reached open water. Then they would raise sail in all their boats and head to the northwest, going into the Bransfield Strait between the mainland and the long chain of islands which were named the South Shetland Islands by the whaler William Smith of ship *The Williams* in 1819. Their main destination would be the warm springs of Deception Island in this group which had been our snug harbour months ago. From there they could press on further north towards the Falkland Islands in the hope that they would meet a ship travelling east through the well-used Drake Passage.

Having rounded the big island, we set sail for Deception Island which according to the old whaling maps should only be about sixty nautical miles to our northeast; a good one-day sail for a fully-rigged ship. The poor *Australis,* however was only now carrying one third of her compliment and few of us were topmen. With such a depleted crew, we had set only our two gibs, and the big spanker[1] which would give us more manoeuvrability and

---

[1] The gibs are the triangular sails which run from the foremast to the bowsprit at the front of the ship. The spanker is a gaff-rigged fore-and-aft sail set from and aft of the aftmost mast.

could be handled from the deck but with a slower rate of knots. However, with the wind now backing again from the south and freshening, I took a chance of hoisting our main topsail in the hope of gaining more speed whilst running before the wind. With few topmen in our small band, I reluctantly climbed with Isaac Townley, our only topman and two others up the ratlines and out on the yards of our mainmast to unfurl the topsail whilst the others below hauled on the port and starboard sheets once the sail had been released. Our little crew though it a point of humour to see their captain climbing the mast as a common sailor and many a rib was jabbed and a finger pointed at my ineptitude aloft.

The day had become one of routine. The cloud was again high, the sky completely overcast and the wind from the south now rated as a moderate breeze. White caps were beginning to form on the top of the waves which I estimated were about six feet in height. Our small crew were happy enough; this was what they were used to and considered as a good day, despite the icy wind. There was nothing between us and Deception Island except open sea and it was probable that we would reach it by the next morning. None-the-less, I had a double watch made up so that we would not run aground on the islands to our north. As Captain, I usually did not stand a watch but I went up on deck several times during the night to both take any star sightings and to give some encouragement to the men. Going on watch at night in bitterly cold weather was never a joy to any man, regardless of how much he loved the sea.

The second watch starting at midnight for four hours was usually the worst. I had had the men of the first watch wake me so that I might see the set of the sail and to take a sight on any of the stars of the southern sky which might be visible. The night was cold, our ship sailed on in an orderly fashion and there were no stars to be seen.

Next day early in the forenoon watch, the dim light of the sun through the high cloud showed Deception Island dead ahead. The wind was still blowing at about fifteen knots from the south and having made one pass of the opening to the interior of the island and seeing no sign of life, I ordered that the mainsail be furled and the ship put about into the wind. We dropped the gibs, secured the spanker fore-and aft and put out a sea anchor from our bow which now faced into the wind. This anchor consisted of three oars lashed together as a triangle and a piece of canvas stretched over the frame and tied strongly, the anchor being attached to a long line secured at our bow. A small can of fish oil was tied to the frame and a hole punctured in it to allow a small amount of oil to seep out. The theory being that the anchor would stay embedded in the sea and we could adjust the anchor line so that the ship rode evenly with each wave. The fish oil would thin and spread out past and surrounding the ship and help to flatten the waves. This seemed to work well and the deck became a little more stable. The secured spanker would keep the ship headed into the wind

Using the mainmast as a support, I examined the entrance and northerly headland of Deception Island. If the other members of the crew had made it to our old camp inside, then there was sure to be a lookout upon that headland. Alas, there was neither sign of any lookout nor any smoke from a signal fire which would be set to attract our attention.

Krystof, that experienced hand had volunteered to take two other men and sail our little whaleboat through the entrance of the island and into the caldera lake beyond. They would land at our old camp and look for any survivors. The men lowered our only whaleboat with her mast rigged and soon Krystof had her sailing spritely through the swell. It was a great sight to see such good sail handling and soon he altered course and headed straight through the narrow entrance called Neptune' Bellows.

Most of the men stayed on deck, eagerly looking to the tall, red cliffs that formed the headlands to the entrance. It was well over two hours when the lookout at the masthead shouted "Sail Ho! They'r a comin out!". The men who had now lapse into a torpor of boredom looked up and gave a loud "Hurrah!" and within the hour were helping Kristof and his men over the side. He came up to where I was standing and knuckled his forehead.

"I um zorry, Capitan. No one wuz there you zee zo we huv come back."

"Thankee Krystof." I said, clapping him on the shoulder, "that was a brave effort. Please tell Lars that you and your men can have an extra tot of rum tonight. We all appreciate what you did."

There was nothing to do here, so we hauled in the sea anchor and went about, raising the gibs and again running before the wind. I had been looking at another map in father's gifted collection and found a more detailed survey of the South Shetland group drawn up by George Powell, the commander of the sloop *Dove* in 1821. It clearly showed the next major island, Livingston's Island, clearly already in view was a mere ten nautical miles to our north. If Caleb Warren and the rest of the crew had got this far and could not negotiate the Bellows as Krystof had done, then this would be the next destination. With a consistent southerly wind, the best anchorage would be around the northern part of the island. Consulting Powell's map, I found that there was a broad, open bay on the north side of the island through what was labelled McFarlane's Strait. Within this bay was a small, semicircular island which had next to it the pencilled notation of Half Moon Island because of its obvious shape. The opening of this half-moon faced north and that would provide a better anchorage than the wide bay could afford. I marked our course from Deception Island and gave the bearing to our quartermaster at the helm.

As we rounded the point on the eastern end of Livingston's Island my hopes of a safe anchorage were somewhat quelled for the point, named Point Renier on Powell's map, consisted of several upright jagged spires of bare rock which led down abruptly to the sea. Giving them a wide berth as we rounded this point, we saw in the distance our destination of Half Moon Island. This too, seemed to be composed of upright spires of rock on both sides of the small harbour in between. Sharp, bare rock, snow and ice seemed to be the main composition of the island. As a precaution, I sent Lars to the bow with a lead line to sound the depth and gave orders for one of the gibs to be lowered to slow us down as we turned westward into the small bay. I stood by Tobias Henry, our quartermaster who by instinct had taken over the wheel from one of our less experienced hands.

"Very steady as we go, Mr Henry." I cautioned and received a firm reply, "Aye, Sir. Steady it be."
Lars had positioned several of the men along the starboard gun'le to relay his calls as he threw the lead-weighted line in front of the bow and recorded the depth by the number of knots on the line as it hit the bottom and the line passed the hull.

"By tha' mark ten," he called. Ten fathoms[2] or about sixty feet. Quite deep for such a small bay. Perhaps this had been another small volcano in some past age.

---

[2] A nautical unit of depth with one fathom equal to 6 feet or 1.8 metres.

"Captain, Sir!" cried the lookout. "There's be men on the beach!" I was startled at this cry and grabbed a telescope from its shelf in the wheelhouse and climbed up on the deckhouse. Surveying the shore in front of us, I saw a group of men; some waving their arms frantically above their heads and some running down from above the beach to join their comrades. It was Caleb Warren and the rest of the crew. The men of the *Australis* were again reunited.

Chapter Eighteen
Revelation and Restoration
Latitude 62° 35' 24" South, Longitude 59° 54' 36" West
30ºF, light winds 5 knots from the west

I can only imagine how Caleb Warren and the men on shore felt as they saw the *Australis* round that easterly headland of Half Moon Island. It had been our engineer, Hamish Dunsmuir who had first sighted the ship. He later explained to me that he had been prone to sit alone up on the tall ridge of stone which ran up into the interior from the beach. The weather being fine, well fine relative to his cold native Newfoundland, he often sought solitude to smoke his pipe. Looking down the bay towards the penguin rookery at the southern end of the headland, he thought that he saw smoke above the weird orange-coated pinnacles above the rookery. He had stood up and shaded his eyes against the glare of the snow. It was smoke!

"Bi aw thon's holy! Tis tha' *Australis*! he had said to himself and when the bowsprit appeared around the headland he had jumped up and half ran and half stumbled down the ridge to bleak settlement below.

"Tha' *Australis*! Tha' *Australis*!" he had shouted and the men who came out of their snug shelters had wondered at their engineer's sanity.

All looked in the direction of his outstretched arm and saw the apparent apparition of their lost ship now coming around the point. Some jumped up and down and waved their arms and others sank to their knees; the religious thanking their God and the superstitious fearing the ghost of their lost captain. As the ship turned towards them and headed into the bay, it soon became apparent that this was no apparition but the ship itself. The *Australis* had indeed come to save them.

On board, I had given the order to drop the topsail and sail as close to the beach as depth would allow. When Lars, who was testing the depth with the lead line, yelled out that the bottom was beginning to shelve, I ordered all sails dropped and had the quartermaster swing her around into the wind. The anchor was let go and we slowly came to rest not fifty yards from the beach.

The men aboard could hardly contain themselves with joy. Here on this isolated beach were their shipmates, given up for lost in this white wilderness. I ordered the Jolly boat to be lowered and we launched our only whaleboat aboard. All the men who could get into the boats did so except for two who reluctantly accepted my orders to stay aboard as anchor watch to see that the ship did not slip her anchor and run aground. They did so with the understanding that they would be relieved in two hours.

Coming ashore was an emotional reunion of old shipmates who had long since been resigned to never seeing each other again. The men ashore had waded into the icy water to pull our boats ashore and eagerly helped their shipmates up the wide pebble beach. Many tears were shed my some whilst others who were more restrained hugged their friends or vigorously shook their hands. Caleb Warren had been in the forefront of the group and had embraced me in a tight grip.

"Jaimie, Jaimie lad. Is it really you? I can't believe my eyes. It is you. I am sorely glad to see you!" he cried with the hint of tears in his eyes and a look of joy on his craggy face.

"Here I am, Caleb. Just as you see me!" I replied, finding it difficult to be a captain not a little boy again who has been greeted by an old family friend.

Arm in arm we walked up the beach and I looked around at this last refuge of the remainder of my crew. The beach was made up entirely of small, rounded pebbles about one to two inches across of some light grey rock. There was a relatively steep slope just above the waterline where our boats had beached but this slope suddenly flattened out to an extensive berm[1]. The beach was wide and stretched around the entire end of the bay. Patches of snow lay here and there around the beach which led up to a flat area of land which was backed by a sudden circular cliff of snow rising up to a series of small, dark grey rock peaks beyond. There were several small penguins standing nonchalantly

---

[1] A flattened stretch of beach or another bank. In beaches, this often represents the upper limit of the high tide.

at various places along the beach; they seemed nonplussed at the activities of these larger creatures coming off the sea.

As we walked up the beach with the gaggle of happy men holding their comrades or taking excitedly, I first perceived the changes that these remnants of my crew had made. Up on the level section of land, just where the pebble beach had flattened out, the snow had been cleared and a habitat of sorts had been fashioned out of larger rocks. These had obviously been brought from a large, fractured ridge of the same grey rock as the beach which now rose up as an uneven jumble of angular boulders and broken spires further inland. These stones had been piled up into rough walls constructed as three long, separate rectangular structures about twenty-five feet or so long and about six feet wide. On top of each, a whale boat had been upended to form a long, rounded roof. The structures had been built so as to meet at an end to form a wide quadrangle, in the middle of which was a circular fire-pit and cooking area in which a small fire was burning. An awning of sorts covered the end of this quadrangle. It was made from upright and horizontal oars lashed together and covered by sealskins. Each wall of the 'hut' was about three feet high and in the middle of each wall which faced the quadrangle was a small opening about a foot and a half wide which acted as a doorway. These too, were covered with a sealskin. Each of the structures also had a stone chimney in the centre of their outer wall.

"Welcome to our camp," Caleb Warren said with mock formality and he beckoned me to sit down on the crude stone benches which surrounded the fire pit. We were soon joined by the rest of the happy throng who sat or stood around the fire. Some extra wood was brought and added to the fire and several coffee pots and kettles were place around its edge.

"We had to sacrifice one of the boats, you see, Captain," He said, now reverting to his position of first mate and apologising for the boat's loss. "Our fuel stores were soon depleted and we had to resort to breaking the boat up. But we did find an old whaler over on yonder shore which had been left by some earlier ship, so we have enough fuel for a while at least."

Around the fire and with warm, shared cups and bowls of coffee we sat and told our separate stories. The men all listened in silence as we each recounted our tales of survival in this dreaded white land, awesome in its beauty and full of wonderful creatures but totally hostile to man.

As captain, the men insisted on my telling my own story of my time alone onboard the *Australis*. They moaned and showed great emotion when I recounted my feelings of loneliness, my forced move to the galley and my inability to keep the deck free of ice. They laughed at my dramatic telling of the tale about the nameless horror who had rattled my door and how I had been ready to defend myself with

The beach on Half Moon Island

The old whaler found on Half Moon Island

my pistol. A lone voice from some old hand who had known me as a boy, shouted out that I probably would have missed my target anyway had I fired my pistol. More laughter.

I recounted my story emphasising that I had stayed onboard because I had faith in the hull of the *Australis* to resist the ice and out of loyalty to my father. It was an apology of sorts for not coming with them when their fear of being crushed in the ice had forced them to seek safety by leaving the ship. This brought a short spell of guilty silence in the group until Joseph Turling, the second mate spoke up:

"We did not want to leave you on the ship Captain, but the men all feared for their lives as some of these good men had seen their comrades die when the *Aquinnah* was crushed in the ice. We did not feel that we had much choice," then turning to Lars, who sat across the fire, "and it was unfortunate that we lost you in that blizzard when we did. I tried to go back but we feared that we would be lost too so we called until we could speak no longer. You understand?"

This was as close to an apology as I had heard from Joseph Turling; not usually a friendly man but a most efficient seaman.

Lars had beamed across the fire, the firelight shining off his long blond hair so that this and his grimy face made him look every inch the young Viking. "Oh, ya! Dat is alright,

Yoseph!" he replied with good nature, and the men laughed at his innocent reply. Lars then took up his tale and told of his snow cave which received many comments of encouragement from his men who held the big Norwegian in great esteem.

"Well, for our part" continued Caleb Warren "we pushed on through that blizzard and I guess that we were too concerned with making our way and didn't look behind. I'm sorry, too Lars." Adversity made all men equal.

The first mate then continued his tale of their march northward. They had stopped in the blizzard and had sought shelter in their boats. Turling and his men had come up to them and did the same. The next morning, with the blizzard cleared they were distressed to see no sign of Lards and his two boats. Turling had retraced his steps until he was almost out of sight of the others and, seeing no sign of the other boats returned. They had marched on together for several more days, hauling the four boats over pressure ridges and avoiding patches of false snow above long crevasses. Eventually they came to a long, narrow lead of open water which led to the north and so they launched their boats. It was often hard going as the lead often narrowed but then it suddenly opened up into a wide stretch of water which extended north to the vague horizon. Setting sail in each of the whalers, the small flotilla headed northeast and after several days hard sailing, they came within sight of Deception Island. The wind had swung around from the west and had freshened to about twenty knots in the strait between the islands and the mainland further east. Mr Turning had taken his boat into the entrance of Neptune's Bellows but found that he did not have enough room to tack and force an entry to the central lagoon. In desperation, Caleb Warren had taken the boats north in the hope of finding a safe anchorage for the coming night. Having copies of my maps, they headed for the wide bay of Livingston's Island which was only about fifteen nautical miles to the northeast[2]. Entering this wide bay that was sheltered from the wind, they had fortuitously sailed into the inlet of Half Moon Island. Here they found the wide beach of pebbles and the ridge of rocks beyond. Because of its northward-facing outlook and protection from the southerly and westerly winds, the beach and some of its surroundings were relatively free of snow. Moreover, there was a large penguin rookery on the headland with several seals. The men had set up the shelters under the first mate's instructions as he had seen such shelters made in the far north during the cruise of the ill-fated *Aquinnah*. In one of their hunting expeditions for seals and penguin eggs, one man had discovered a rich supply of thick green moss. Whilst this was fairly neutral to the taste, the first mate had used this plant in an attempt to forestall scurvy, the early symptoms of which had begun to appear amongst some of the men. With a secure camp, the men had settled down to a routine of survival. Seals were hunted and their skins were used as coverings, their meat for food and their blubber for fuel in the few small oil lamps which were

---

[2] About 28 kilometres.

fashioned out of ration tins. With the weather becoming colder and windier, ideas of a quick passage to safety further north had begun to dwindle and an air of melancholy had fallen over the camp. When the *Australis* had appeared around the point everything changed.

Around the fire, the huddle of men exchanged their own personal stories of surviving the fearsome march across the ice and then the long, wind-swept and spray-filled voyage across the rough, open sea. It was time to go.

"Time to get onboard, men." I said in a loud voice to gain their attention. "Let us restore the whalers to their original purpose and get on board the *Australis* to a nice warm foc'sle and some proper vittles."

There were universal cries of approval and the men broke up into little groups to breakdown their crude, stone huts, turn the boats back up to their normal position and to load whatever supplies that were useful as well as the few personal belongings which they had brought with them.

During this activity, Mr Dunsmuir the engineer came up to me. "Begging yer pardon, captain, kin ah speak wi' ye?"

"Certainly, Mr Dunsmuir," I replied with a smile.

"Ah hae a mynd tae fix oor goosed propellor. Ye see, th' tide is gey lairge 'ere abouts 'n' we cuid run th' stern o' th' ship up oan th' beach at heich tide 'n' then we cuid git tae th' proppellor." He said with the earnest candour of the true engineer.

"Will you get enough exposure to our screw to fix the damage?" I queried.

"Och aye! it wull be heich tide in a oor or twa 'n' if we cuid git her stern oan th' beach we wull git tae th' propellor a' richt," came his emphatic reply.

The plan to put the stern of the *Australis* up on the beach and repair the propeller seemed most practical. It would help us get out of this bay for already I had noticed that several large ice floes had drifted around the point driven by the cold southerly wind.

"Very good, Mr Dunsmuir. Make it so." And I turned to find Caleb Warren and Joseph Turling who would be needed to turn the ship around and bring her stern up onto the broad pebble beach.

Told of our plan, most of the men stayed on the beach with Mr Turling, happy that there was a chance to fix our damaged propeller. The others took two of the whalers and went aboard the *Australis* to turn the ship stern on to the beach. This was done in the light breeze by hoisting the anchor and one of the jibs. With the wheel at full lock and the gib swung over, the ship slowly turned so that its bow now faced out of the bay. The gib and the anchor were again dropped but the anchor line was not secured and so that it would play out when the ship was hauled towards the beach. Two stout ropes were attached to the stern bollards[3] on either side of the stern wheelhouse. These were taken ashore so that the men could then slowly haul the ship to the waterline of the beach at the highest tide. This came within the hour and the *Australis* was pulled up to the beach stern first. Having thus secured the ship on the beach, we waited until the tide receded. This would take about six hours, so the men went about restoring their berths in the foc'sle and John Stevens, our young second engineer took some men and rebuilt one section of one of the stone enclosures into a small fire pit which could be used as a blacksmith's furnace. For this purpose, he had brought several bags of coal and a large bellows used in the engine room to start the boiler fires.

It took only four hours for the propeller shaft and its housing to be exposed. Dunsmuir and his assistant inspected them and the engineer came over to where I had been watching the activity.

"Och, it's nae as ill as ah though bit nae guid either mynd. Th' propellor is guid enough, blades a bawherr bit bent, bit yin o' th' guides whilk ur used tae raise 'n' lower it's buckled." he reported with the grave look that all practical men have when faced with any problem.

"Can it be fixed, Mr Dunsmuir?" I enquired.

---

[3] A sturdy, short, vertical post used principally for mooring ships.

"Och aye, bit it wull likelie jam as soon as we raise th'
propellor th' foremaist time. It wull hae tae be taken aff 'n'
straighted in yon furnace. It'll tak' loads hours," was his
gruff reply.

"Very good, Mr Dunsmuir. I am sure that you and Mr
Stevens will have it fixed before then. We have a large
number of ice floes coming into the bay and I fear that it
will probably ice up at nightfall," I said, pointing out into
the bay.

"That we wull dae Captain. Ah dinnae wantae spend mah
time frozen 'ere again," he said, turning away and yelling
commands to his stokers who were now unbolting one of
the long rails which acted as guides to raise and lower the
coupling through which the propeller rotated.

My fears about being frozen in again were shared by many
of the men and Mr Warren who had come to me as soon as
I returned onboard the *Australis*.

"I don't much like the look of the sea, Captain Jaimie. I fear
we are in for the real start of winter now and we will be
frozen in again."

"It doesn't look good, Caleb," I admitted, "but Mr
Dunsmuir assured me that he can fix the propeller, then
with the aid of our engine and some of the sails we should

be able to push through that pack at the mouth of the bay and head into open water before nightfall."

Dunsmuir and his men worked frantically, hammering the twisted iron guide flat on a large boulder which they had rolled down from the broken ridge behind the beach. Mr Stevens had fired up the makeshift furnace and had heated the guide to red heat. They took it in turns hammering the guide with even engineer Dunsmuir impatiently swinging the hammer at times. Soon the guide was straightened and cooled in the cold air so that it would not fracture. With the tide again rising, they positioned the guide onto its wooden supporting frame at the stern, matched its companion and bolted it home with the propeller housing freely moving within it. A liberal smearing of tallow was added to the entire length of the guides to help this movement.

Picking up their tools and belongings, the engineer called out to me where I was standing above at the stern rail, "Tis a' dane, noo captain. We hae a ship again!"

I laughed at the thought that all engineers think that a ship is incomplete without an engine. In their mind, the engineers and the stokers ran the entire ship; the rest of the crew, the mast and sails being simply mere passengers and cargo.

With the wind now freshening and coming over the southern ridge of the island, we hoisted our fore and aft sails and I gave orders for our engine to be started.

Dunsmuir's stokers had raised steam in the boilers before we had come aboard and now, we tried passing it into our engine. Dunsmuir was cautious and there was no motion of the ship as yet. The vibration of the engine showed me that it was at least in working order; but for how long we were not too sure. There was some additional vibration at the stern which was to be expected with a misshapen propeller but the tell-tale wash at the stern reassured me that everything was as the engineer had expected. Soon we were gliding out of the bay of Half Moon Island and heading through the thin ice pack. The sea now had its glazed look with tiny cracks running this way and the next as the surface froze then was broken up by the water currents. Luckily the main mass of floes had not yet been pushed up from beyond the southern point of the island and as the dim sun began to set, we sailed eastward and came into the main channel. Here it was relatively ice-free with just a few small icebergs and larger floes close into the islands to our west. These were named the South Shetland Islands, from here our course would be northeast until we rounded the last of them and then headed due north to the Falkland Islands and civilisation. We would take on coal and stores and see to our many small repairs before heading north up through the Atlantic to home.

Chapter Nineteen
Reflections on the Sea

Latitude 14° 47' 24" South, Longitude 26° 46' 48' West
70ºF, light winds 5 knots from the South

It had been many weeks now since the *Australis* had broken free from its icy prison. We had sailed her in a partly repaired state to Port Stanley in the Falklands where we were greeted with much sympathy and friendliness by its inhabitants. The propeller mounting had finally received a professional repair and the crew had seen to the repairs to our masts, spars and sails. By the time we had left the port, our good ship had been restored to something akin to her former glory. Not so the men.

It had been a hard voyage and experience for many of the men. Some of them had endured imprisonment in the ice for a least a second time and now had a fear of such icy places. Many of the older hands had vowed that they would give up whaling entirely and retire to some nice New England farm well away from the sea. The younger hands had suddenly become older experienced hands and now had a greater respect for the sea and how cruel she could be. More so for her handmaiden, ice. They would go to sea again and brave the waves that rolled across the North Atlantic. They would steer their ship through ice floes and hunt the great whale, continuing a trade which was their only way. For the sailorman has both a love and hate for the sea. He will grumble when he is shaken out of his hammock to go on the second watch at midnight but will fret if he is beached and put ashore for any length of time.

For my part, I have learned many lessons during the voyage of the *Australis*, my first command. I have seen the great whale in her own land; her place of refuge during the summer months; her natural curiosity in a place where she is queen and where mankind is not to be feared. In her domain too, are all of the other creatures who live in their icy Antarctic home. There are the smaller whales such as the ferocious Orca, the gentle Minke and the playful dolphins. There are the great variety of seals, the canines of the ice; some gentle and others dangerous in their intent, but all curious. There are the polite and fussy penguins who on land waddle about like diminutive butlers in their black and white jackets but in the water dart about faster than any fish. Other birds also inhabit these regions; the blue-eyed cormorants who sit on rock ledges or fly above in their graceful formations and the deceptive Snowy Sheathbill, white as the snow in which it hides. Of the Antarctic birds, the most feared by the smaller creatures is the great hunter, the Skua, with a wingspan wider than a man's outstretched arms and a curved beak designed to crush penguin eggs and small penguins alike.

We were now several days out of Rio heading due north, with only the slightest of wind behind us but taking us home. The men had taken a well-earned leave in that vibrant city, both from the sea and the boredom of shipboard routine. I had come up on deck well into the second watch as I had found sleep difficult now in the stifling heat of tropical waters. For a while I stood in the small wheelhouse aft, receiving the slightest nod from the helmsman who was intent on the movement of the line within the binnacle[1] and keeping our course with the occasional glance to the stars above as though the compass, old as its use may be, was still not to be trusted.

I moved over to the rail and glanced up at our full set of sails; the aft mainsail flapped occasionally, like some prime stallion wishing to shake off its bridle and run free and the huge wall of the spanker which would suddenly swing over from one side to the next on its shortened course. There was little wind in our sails and even less across the water. The sea was almost at a dead calm; the water like a mass of glassy hills, heaving ever so slightly and reflecting the shiny canopy above. The stars were myriad in their number and of brightness and colour never seen on land; whites, blues, orange and reds. I looked astern and could make out the Southern Cross, that great constellation that now had dipped well-nigh the distant horizon. I looked down over the side and saw the fluorescence of the hull moving through the black, starry sea. All was quiet around the ship except for the occasional flap of the sails and gentle clanging of some tormented rigging. It was a great time for reflection.

---

[1] The round brass housing containing the ship's compass. The line is the Lubber's Line of the compass glass which is to be kept on the course assigned.

In retrospect, father's great plan for our Antarctic voyage had been an overall failure. We had not caught many whales and our store of oil had been almost depleted by the necessities of our survival. Antarctica had been even more foreboding than Arctic waters which had been well-known to most of our crew. The sheer vastness of the place, its hammering winds which penetrated the best of clothing and shelter with its intense cold, and its deadly ice which came upon us suddenly and without mercy. Antarctica was both a region totally inhospitable to mankind as it was dangerously beautiful. Ice, our greatest foe was also a creature of wonder. Totally beautiful in its many forms of translucency and its many hues of blue and white, it covered the rocks of the land and spread its mantle across the sea. Drifting ice, sometimes flat as a secure home to the penguin and seal and at other times of great proportions as icebergs which easily dwarfed our little ship. Completely unfit for humans, this awesome land was still home to a great many forms of life which had adapted to living in such severe conditions both in the air, on its rocky and icy shores and especially within the sea.

It had not been a successful whaling voyage because we had approached it from the wrong way thinking. Our New England way of hunting the great whale in small boats from the mother ship did not work well in a place where the cold winds blew the waves into icy walls and ice-filled seas restricted our passage but gave our quarry plenty of scope for hiding. We had also sailed too far to the south. Perhaps in more northern waters around the Falklands we may have used our good ship to its full potential, but the locals there had told us that whaling was very much a common occupation in their waters and the great whale was even becoming scarce there about. Whaling, of course would continue. There were too many people dependent upon the bounty given up by the great whale; oil for their lamps, spermaceti for candles, baleen for ribs of corsets and other supports and meat for consumption. There may come a time when smaller, steam-powered hunting ships may be stationed in secure harbours such as ours in Deception Island[2] or even associated with a larger vessel which could be used as a factory ship with much more processing than the modest operations aboard the *Australis*. Such a plan for future whaling had already been the talk around the table with Peder Andersen and father when we had been in Bergen, but then my attentions were only for the lovely Liv Andersen, Peder's daughter and assistant.

As my thoughts wandered on that warm, starry night, I thought more of that lovely Norwegian girl and of the future. I had lost my desire to go on more icy voyages after the whale in the Arctic, and despite the beauty of the place, the Antarctic was no longer attractive to me. The Australis had been the only success of our current voyage. The harsh conditions of the Antarctic seas had shown the value of Peder Andersen's foresight and skill. Perhaps the days of

---

[2] The bay within Deception Island in which the *Australis* sheltered was later called Whaler's Bay and was indeed a site for a permanent whaling station. It had long been a shelter for sealing expeditions since the 1820's and the whaling station was set up here in the early 1900's but was destroyed by an eruption of the volcano in 1969 and abandoned.

sail may be over and it will be the steamship which will dominate the oceans of the future. Time will tell for the steamship also relies upon the vast stores of coal which would have to be placed at strategic ports around the world of trade. Ships like the *Australis*, with its engine, strengthened hull, steam heating and powered winches could go anywhere, especially if the engines became more reliable and the propellers more protected. I thought about the future and was determined that I should take the Tobey Whaling Company into the wider world of trade. We had the ability to use the *Australis*, with its great storage capacity to carry all manner of goods to and from the American shores to exotic ports unable to be serviced by sail due to the winds. We would have Andersen build us another ship, more powerful in steam than my current command and able to steam anywhere in the world. My mind soared at the prospect of the steam ships of the future whilst the sails continued to flap overhead. My mind also wandered again to Bergen, that beautiful port in Norway where my lovely Liv Andersen resided. We had taken up a very regular correspondence when the *Australis* had left her shipyard in Bergen and I had eagerly looked forward to the weekly post in New Bedford. Her letters had been long and sweet sounding; sweet smelling too, for she had usually scented them with a subtle but wondrous perfume which reminded me of the flowers we had picked in the mountain forest which had overlooked her home. There had been a sort of understanding between us and I think that father and Peder Andersen thought it too, that perhaps the two families would one day unite. This is what I would propose when we reached home. For now, I would rest on the rails of my dear ship and breathe in the warm air of the tropical South Atlantic and think of wondrous things which will come about in the future. The *Australis* was again a lively ship sailing through a calm ocean and no longer the white ice ship of the Antarctic.

Epilogue
27° 28' 12.45" South and 153° 1' 15.86' East
72⁰F, light winds 7 knots from the West Southwest

This book is a work of fiction and the characters within it are also fictional. Most of the places mentioned in the story and some of the events are real and some of the events have been based on my own experience.

I have never commanded a ship at sea but have been an Officer/Instructor in the Australian Naval Cadets for over twelve years and commanded one of their local units of some fifty cadets. I have also had a very short time at sea with the navy and six training cruises aboard Tall Ships, both square-rigged and schooner rigged. I learned aboard these craft that a sailor in such vessels had a hard but very satisfying life. Responding to 'all hands aloft to shorten sail!' I know what it is like to be shaken out of a warm bunk at some ungodly hour of the night to quickly throw on some warm clothes and join my watch struggling up the ratlines on the main mast and then out along the thin foot-ropes of the yard arm to fold up the wet, cold and very stiff sail which flapped in a strong breeze. It was cold enough doing this in the Tasman Sea in sub-tropical waters, but to do this in weather which was below freezing and in an Antarctic gale would be an amazing feat of strength, endurance and willpower. 'One hand to the ship and one for yourself' was the rule, but this was often not possible, so locking one's knees to stop the legs shaking with cold and fear and bodily hanging over the yard was often the only alternative. On one occasion, our schooner did dip its bow deep into an oncoming roller and one of our crew went under as described. I ran aft along the deck with a metre of water following.

Bergen is a beautiful port city in south western Norway. My wife and I spent some time there, especially out and about the old waterfront and up the funicular railway to the forested mountains above the town. Here we did find a structure in the rock which looked remarkably like a sad faced troll, caught unexpectedly in the morning sunlight and turned into rock. The character of Liv Andersen is based upon my wife whom I met onboard a ship. She is the daughter and was sometime assistant of an engineer specialising in steam boilers. During a tour of our cruise ship's engine room, she astounded the ship's engineer by informing him there was a problem with one of the boilers. This was meant to be a secret that he and the Captain were keeping from the passengers. Forty-five years later, and with a Physics Degree amongst others, she is still my travelling companion into some of the most inhospitable places such as the glaciers of New Zealand and the Andes, down the Amazon by canoe, across the Nubian Desert by bus, the Rockies and Alaska, and various volcanoes but not Antarctica because she hates the cold.

I have also ventured down the Antarctic Peninsular in a small ship which was once built as a research vessel for such waters and then later converted for eco-tourism. With crew and passengers about eighty, the M.V. *Usuhaia* was a wonderful little ship, totally unlike the larger cruise liners which also took paying passengers south. Because of our small size and the adventurous nature of our Argentinian crew, we were able to safely push into places where the larger vessels would never go. We also pushed the limits of our own endurance but at no time did I ever feel that I was in danger. This of course was an illusion for there was danger all around. The only time in which there was a small feeling of fear creeping into my mind was when our small, five metre rubber zodiac boat was at some great distance from the ship, in the shallows and the sea had started to freeze as described in the book in Chapter 8 when we went to look at the wreck of the *Guvernøren*[1] in Foyn Harbour at 64°33′ South 62°1′ West. If the sea had completely frozen, we would not have been able to return to the ship, and being in the shallows of the harbour, she would not have been able to come to us. Luckily, our experienced Argentinian coxswain solved the problem by revving the outboard and jumping the dinghy over the smaller floes. Here too, we found the old whale boat as described in that chapter, embedded into the ice wall opposite the wreak. The coxswain mentioned that there was a rumour that the bow of this whale boat, now embedded in the ice, contained barrels of gunpowder. We also took our small ship through Neptune's Bellows into the caldera of Deception Island with the idea of going swimming in the hot springs there.

---

[1] This was a Norwegian whaling factory ship which was scuttled on 27 January, 1915 after a fire on board threatened its valuable cargo of whale oil. The tale was that there had been a good party onboard. The rusted hulk of this steel vessel now acts as an anchorage site for intrepid sailors.

Unfortunately, the wind was too strong to launch our zodiacs so we had to be content with looking at Whaler's Bay and its wrecked whaling station through binoculars. We did land at Half Moon Island with its pebble beach as described in Chapter Eighteen and had a good look around. There were buildings of the mothballed Argentinian base, *Camera* and the surroundings looked suitable for such a camp as described in that chapter. There was a large penguin rookery closer to the headland of the bay and the beach and rocky ridge behind it were relatively free of ice. Several seals were also noticed and there would have been good fishing in the bay. A long ridge of sharp, rocky spires and peaks sheltered this bay from the southerly and westerly winds. It was also the first time in two weeks that we had seen direct sunlight and there was a carpet of green moss in a wet but north-facing sheltered position.

Many of the descriptions of the wildlife and their icy habitat have also come from firsthand experience. We did have a humpback whale dive under the ship and in Foyn Harbour we also had two fifteen metre Minke whales come up to our small zodiac and then circle it. Had the water been warmer, I could have touched one as it swum past our thin rubber hull. These whales are relatively peaceful but curious and could have easily upturned our small craft, even accidentally. There were also Orcas or killer whales about, we also watched a pod of three circle a small ice floe on which stood three small Adélie penguins. They stood perfectly still whilst the Orcas passed; had the whales seen the birds, they would have rapidly circled the floe until it upturned. Penguins are remarkable birds; waddling along in line like a class of trainee butlers on land but as swift as torpedoes under the water. They are curious animals and did not respect the five metre distance that we humans were given when confronting them. They really did have a well-governed road system of up and down tracks between their rookeries and the sea. It was a joy to watch them moving up and down and the occasional non-conformist going up the down track. This bird would have to stand aside when confronted with a line of its fellows coming down. There was always a solitary resident Skua bird nearby the penguin rookery. These birds preyed on penguin eggs and small penguins. One did not like our presence and dive-bombed us in our zodiac. With a wingspan of well over a metre and a very sharp beak, this was most disconcerting!

Seals were usually alone or in some rare instance in pairs. Crabeater seals, Weddell seals, Elephant Seals and Leopard seals were all encountered but kept at a distance for we were warned that to get between a seal and the sea could invoke an attack. Leopard seals, being carnivores were the most dangerous.

Eric the Red, or Jeger, as Lars the carpenter would call him, the Norwegian Forest Cat is based on our own cat who is as described in the book in Chapter Twelve. A very large and intelligent cat, Anthony is more of a watchdog than a cat. He is a great hunter and will often bring in his live prey in the wee small hours with a distinctive cry of urgency for me to get up and receive this offering to our kitchen larder. These poor animals include mice, rats, baby possums, birds, geckos and small snakes. Often, he will release them when I stagger into the hallway where he is guarding these hapless creatures. There then occurs another frantic hunt around the house until the prey is again caught. Snakes are the main problem as even baby snakes of about 30-40 centimetres can be poisonous. I usually capture these animals and release them outside later. Over time, Anthony has learned that only the obnoxious introduced geckos earn a reward of a cat treat and so these are now his only prey. Whilst Leopard seals are in short supply here in sub-tropical suburbia, Anthony keeps watch on our front yard and will attack any dog that is foolish enough to intrude. Two large Alsatian dogs were his last victims.

I have tried to write this book as if it has been truly written by a young whaling captain and have attempted to follow the sort of wonder given in Jules Verne's *Voyages Extraordinaires,* but I do not claim that I have his talent. Set in the 1840's, such a ship as the Australis would have been futuristic in its concept and many of its features, such as steam heating, raiseable propeller and power winches were not to appear until at least fifty years later. The *Australis* is based upon many ships, especially those of the great Antarctic explorers, Shackleton, Mawson, Scott and many others at the beginning of the 20th Century. The idea of a crush-proof wooden hull with the ability to drift within the frozen pack-ice came from that of the construction of the *Fram,* Fridtjof Nansen's famous ship in which he and his crew drifted across the Arctic Sea trapped in its ice. This ship was also used by Roald Amundsen in his southern polar expedition from 1910 to 1912. I was in the Antarctic waters exactly one hundred years to the day since Roald Amundsen reached the South Pole on 14th December 1911, five weeks ahead of a British party led by Robert Falcon Scott. On board the *Ushuaia*, the group of young Norwegians who were there to celebrate this event, did so with an elaborate cake and champagne provided by the Argentinians who always enjoy a good party. They were most happy to hear that there also was a Scott attending their celebration, even though he was no relation to that famous explorer who had bravely lost the race to the Pole.

I must say that I do not support the world-wide whaling industry and if it is to be maintained at all, it should be limited to those indigenous peoples who have traditionally hunted the whale for their own purposes or at most whaling should be done only in the home waters of the whaling countries.

Antarctica is now a wilderness area governed by countries which have signed the Antarctic Treaty in 1959. This treaty prohibits military activities and mineral mining, prohibits nuclear explosions and nuclear waste disposal, supports scientific research, and protects the continent's environment. Scientific research stations there must be active, pending activity or totally removed. Although eco-tourism is becoming popular, there are strict rules governing the activities of ships going south. Generally, smaller ships with a limited number of tourists fare better than large cruise ships which have restraints on the number of tourists allowed to land at any given place. Hopefully, habitation, no matter how temporary will continue to be controlled because of the problems with the environment. On that issue, Antarctica is also suffering from the effects of global warming due to the excessive use of fossil fuels and ocean pollution, especially from dissolved carbon dioxide which produces ocean acidity, increased ocean heat which melts ice as well as providing better breeding grounds for bacteria and other parasites which have begun to impact with the wildlife there. An overall view of global warming and climate change is given in my non-fiction work, ADVENTURES in EARTH and ENVIRONMENTAL SCIENCE (Felix Publishing 2019).

Dr. Peter T. Scott
Brisbane, August 2019.

www.ingramcontent.com/pod-product-compliance
Lightning Source LLC
Chambersburg PA
CBHW070621170726
48291CB00003B/825